Dark Dynasty Thy Cursed Family Legacy

By
Bernadette Carington

Illustrations by
Mina Anne Poe & Ariana Coleen Dolan

PITTSBURGH, PENNSYLVANIA 15238

The contents of this work including, but not limited to, the accuracy of events, people, and places depicted; opinions expressed; permission to use previously published materials included; and any advice given or actions advocated are solely the responsibility of the author, who assumes all liability for said work and indemnifies the publisher against any claims stemming from publication of the work.

All Rights Reserved
Copyright © 2016 by Bernadette Carington

No part of this book may be reproduced or transmitted, downloaded, distributed, reverse engineered, or stored in or introduced into any information storage and retrieval system, in any form or by any means, including photocopying and recording, whether electronic or mechanical, now known or hereinafter invented without permission in writing from the publisher.

RoseDog Books
585 Alpha Drive
Suite 103
Pittsburgh, PA 15238
Visit our website at *www.rosedogbookstore.com*

ISBN: 978-1-4809-7172-1
eISBN: 978-1-4809-7149-3

Dedication

I would like to dedicate this book to my friends, and fans. Thank you for all of the support, the words of wisdom and encouragement.

This is also for all of the people, that helped me make my dream come true.

And last but not least my dear friends Sheba, Babette, Mindy, Victoria, and Inna. And very special loving thank you to my daughter Angelina. This one is for you with love.

Story Introduction

This story takes place in Wales in the small town of Carington Point.

It is a town that I made up for this story. If it did in fact exist, it would be near the port town of Cardiff. It is a small town that consists of textile plants, and quaint shops. In the day time it seems like a typical town, but at night it is far from normal.

Bernadette's First Diary Entry

I'm Bernadette Carington and this is my story. I am a vampire and not by my own will ether! My maker is an evil vampire named Adrian. I arrived from the past. And now I'm currently living here, in the modern times. In a little town my family named Carington Point.

Dark Dynasty
Part 1

Torment Thy Name is Bernadette

Before I came to Carington Point I decided, to transform myself into a cat. I thought that I might as well look around before I proceeded toward the old house. I walked through town, to see if there were any differences between my time and theirs. The only difference was the mode of transportation. When I had seen enough I went behind a small shop, and when I came back out of the shadows. I had transformed myself into a black cat, I called Bella Noir the name was on the tag of my dark red collar. I had now began my long walk to the old house. Stopping ever so often to rest and find something to eat. Or in my case some blood to drink. I came upon a mouse it was just enough, to take me half way there. My feet were starting to hurt so I decided to fly the rest of the way. I turned into Corina the crow and flew the rest of the way. When I got there Charles was leaving the house, he had left a window open. I flew inside, where I then returned to my former self; and stared to walk around. To get a feeling of my surroundings. I made myself comfortable, after I had rested for a while; I flew out the window.

    Once I had my fill I returned to the house. When I got back my watcher was waiting inside, her name is Willamina Adams, "Your room is ready master." "Thank you Willa I will see you later," then I went to my room. While Willa made her way to hers. To clean up after her long trip. When suddenly there was a knock at the door. It was Charles, Willa went to the door to see who it was. All of a sudden it opened and in walked Charles. "Who are you? No one is supposed to be here!" "Then way are you here?" "I live in the main house, I come here to get away from the madness; of my family. My name is Charles O' Shaughnissy. And what is your name?" "Willamina Adams, but you can call me Willa."

"Then you can call me Charlie." Well Charlie my mistress is sleeping. "She is very tired after our long trip as am I. I'm sorry but I am going to have to ask you to leave." "What is her name may I ask?"

"It's Bernadette Carington, she is named after her grandmother." "I will let you get some rest, then and I will see you later." As soon as she shut the door, Willa called a locksmith; to change the locks on the doors and widows of the house. After she paid him for his services, Willa then placed a note on the door that read, Please do not Disturb. Then she called every utility company, she needed to and had all of them put under her name. She resumed to make her way to her room to rest. Meanwhile things were not as calm at the other house. Edward and his sister Rachel, were talking about the children and how to maintain the household. Charles was fighting with his younger cousin Daniella, and her insisting that there are ghosts in the attic of their house. She claims to have seen at least four of them, while playing up there. She told him that there were two men, one woman and a boy.

That she plays with all the time, because there is no other children in their house for her to play with. Charles told Daniella she was a nut case. Victor had enough of the fighting and yelling. And went in to put a stop to all of it. He asked Daniella, "what are the names of your friends in the attic?"

She told him their names, "they are, Guinevere, Darren, Keith and Joseph." "Who are they?" He asked her? "Darren was married to Guinevere and Keith was their son. Joseph was married to Bernadette, he killed himself after she died." While they were talking, Guinevere and Christine were settling in at the caretakers house. Charles snuck out through the back door, and headed to the gatehouse. He called his girlfriend Katherine, and asked her to meet him at the Blue Moon in an hour. As nightfall came I awoke and came down from my room. Willa was cleaning in the drawing room, when I entered the room. "I'm going out now, please see to it; that no one comes in while I'm gone." Then I went out to hunt, while Willa stayed in and read her book. Charles drove into town to meet Katherine at the pub. When he got there, she was already waiting at the table. That they sat at every time they ate there. "I'm glad you called, I hate staying in on weekends". "Me too he said, my house is full of nut jobs!" She said, "what do you mean?" "Daniella thinks that there are ghosts in our attic."

"Are there ghosts in your house? It is a pretty old house you know." "Please not you too! I don't know if there is or not. I have never seen or even heard them. Victor doesn't help ether." Why do say that? "He believes her, and he wants her to take him up there; to meet them himself." Back at the house Victor went up to the attic, with Daniella to see her friends; that live up there. As they were heading up the stairs, there was a knock at the door. Edward answered it, "it's Patricia she is here to see Victor."

"Let her in Edward," Rachel said. Patricia asked, is Victor here? Rachel said, "yes he is up in the attic with Daniella." May I go and see them? "Yes you may, Edward will you take her up?" "Alright sis," he said rudely. Rachel sat in her chair drinking her tea and reading the paper. Edward came down, he said nothing as he sat down, lit his pipe, drinking his wine. And read the stock reports. Patricia joined Victor and Daniella in the attic. She asked them, what they were doing up there? They told her that they were waiting, for her ghostly friends to appear. She didn't say anything, she just sat there and waited with them. Out back in the caretakers house, Guinevere and Christine were drinking their cups of wolfbane tea. With lemon and honey hoping, that the witch that gave it to them was right.

That it would keep them from turning into, canis larans (ravenous beast). I was heading home from my nightly hunt. When I suddenly came upon the place were, Armand and Adrian were staying. I made sure that they did not see me. I did not want to run into Adrian I hated, him for what he had done to me! I managed to make it home with out them noticing me. When I got home, Willa asked me if I was alright, I told her, I came across the place where Adrian lives. She said, "He didn't see you did he?" "No I made sure of that." "That's good we don't need him coming here!" "No we don't, I'm going to my room." Willa loved working for her master, but she was also lonely. She would love someone to talk to. When Bernadette was either out on a hunt, or sleeping until nightfall. Over at the other house, Victor, Daniella and Patricia were still in the attic. The room suddenly became very cold, Keith appeared. He came to play with Daniella. Keith got scared and was about to disappear. When Daniella told him that it was ok, they were her friends. And that they were not there to make him leave for good. That they just wanted to meet him, and the other ghosts that live in the attic with him. Edward asked, Rachel what they were doing in the attic? Rachel told him that his daughter, believed that there are ghosts in their attic. And that she could see and hear them. He just looked at her and started to laugh, and went back to reading the paper. At the caretakers house Christine and Guinevere looked at the clock, and noticed that the bewitching hour had passed. The tea had worked just as the witch told them it would. Back at the Blue Moon pub, Charles and Katherine were waiting for Nicole to bring them their food. Shane came over to the table, to say hi. And to see if they needed anything, before their order got there. He also wanted to know how his son was. Because he had not seen him for a while. Charles told Shane that Victor was fine. And that he would let him know that his dad had asked about him. After Shane left the table, their order came to them. Nicole asked if they needed anything else?

They said no thank you we're fine. Meanwhile Guinevere and Christine, decided to go for a walk in the night air. As they were walking they came across, Armand and Adrian. They made sure that they did not see them. Adrian was standing over a lifeless woman. Armand did not say anything his face said it all for him. Adrian bent down and slashed his wrist, and put it up to her mouth making her drink his blood. She was shaking violently, when she stopped she stood up. And looked around seeing things she had never seen before. She looked at Adrian and said, "what the hell are you!? And what the hell did you do to me?!" "I'm Adrian I am a vampire, and I'm your maker and now I'm your master." "The hell you are! And who are you? And why in the hell did you, not try and stop him!; From turning me into a blood sucking freak!" "I'm Armand and this beast here is my brother.

I would have stopped him if I had come with him, but I came after he had already bitten you."

"Please kill me I can't live like this!" "If I kill you I would have to wait till you are a sleep. And I would have to drive a stake through your heart, or chop off your head." "Then do it take my head or stab me in the heart! I will not try to stop you, I will never turn anyone into a beast like I am now!" Armand did as she asked and took her life, when he was finished he made her body vanish. Armand gave his brother a look that could kill, it was the look of hate! Then he vanished. Adrian was out raged he was thinking of a way to kill his brother. Then he too vanished and went out to find another victim. Guinevere and Christine headed home, Christine looked at her sister and said.

"I hope that we will never end up like those two." Guinevere said, "we will always remain friends."

The Sheriff got a call, telling him about a fight in the woods. When Sheriff Mc Smith got to the place where the fight occurred there was no one there. And there was no sign of a struggle, or even a body or blood. When he went back to the office, and told the officer that took the call, that he didn't find anything at all. The Sheriff asked, who called it in? He told him, that it was someone that was walking, the path through the woods. The said, "they heard someone screaming and crying, then pleading for someone to kill them. Because the did not want to live, if they were a monster; and that's what they told me sir." "Did they give a name or number?" "No sir they did not, I asked for both; they said no way, and hung up sorry sir." "Your fine it is not your fault, they were probably drunk or stoned or both." Charles and Katherine paid for their dinner, then they went to a movie. Back at the main house, Victor and Patricia left the attic. Leaving Daniella up there with her ghostly friends. Victor told Patricia that he had to make a phone call. While she headed to the bathroom, he went into the den and shut the door. He called his old friend Justin Harrington.

He is an expert on paranormal phenomenons. Victor told him, about the ghosts in the attic. Justin told him that he would come and investigate. Victor told Justin, that he did not want him to remove them. He just wanted to know if they were, evil or friendly. Because Daniella has made friends with them. Justin told, Victor that he would observe the specters before he would decide what to do. Victor left the den and joined Patricia in the hall. They left the house and headed to the Blue Moon for dinner.

While at dinner Patricia asked Victor, about what they saw in the attic. He told her that he called his friend Justin, whom hunts ghosts. And that he would be there in the morning. We will go up later in the evening and take Daniella with us. Patricia told him, that she felt sorry for her. Because she didn't have anyone else to play with except Keith. "She has her dog Katy I gave her for her birthday last year." Nicole came over and took their order. She told them, that his dad was asking about him earlier.

When Charles and Katherine were there earlier that evening. Shane looked over and saw his son, and came over to the table. "Long time no see son."

"Very funny dad," giving his dad a hug. Sean Patricia's dad the other owner of the pub. Came over to the table to see his daughter. As the two men were leaving the table, Nicole came over with their food. After they ate they went to see a movie. They ran into Charles and Katherine, the four of them went to see the same one. Back at the old house, Willa was sitting by the fire reading. I was pacing around. I was very apprehensive. Knowing something was wrong, I didn't say a word;

grabbed my cape and left. Turning into Corina, I flew to the main house then entered the attic. I cloaked myself, by using my thoughts I called my husbands spirit. Joseph then appeared, I told him to come with me. He asked me if I were a ghost? I lied to him and said yes. I also told him that someone was coming to remove the spirits from the house for good. And that we would be apart again, so he went with me. I took him to the old house, when we got there. Willa was happy for me. But she was also mad because she had no one for herself. I lead Joseph's spirit to the room next to mine. I told him that I would be right back. I went downstairs to talk to Willa. I told her to have our carriage driver take her into town. Have dinner at the Blue Moon, and see a play afterwords, I will see you later. Please be very careful, do not let Adrian see you. Here Willa take one of my cloaking capes to keep you safe. Willa did as she was told and left for the evening. I went back up stairs to see Joseph. Willa did not end up alone for long. The D.S. Albert Jones came into eat and saw her sitting all alone. He asked if he could sit with her? She said yes, as the evening was winding down all of the young couples were heading home. All except Willa and Albert they were going to a play. Charles took Katherine home, and Victor took Patricia back to the Blue Moon. After the play was finished, Willa said goodnight to Albert, got into the carriage cloaked herself and headed home.

 Albert did the same as he was going, home he thought to himself. I hope I will see her again. Victor and Charles got home at the same time. At the caretakers house the to sisters, were coming back from their nightly walk. They were sitting and talking, Guinevere told Christine she felt like something bad was going to happen! Her sister asked, what she thought it was? She said, "someone is coming to vanquish, the spirits from the main house." Christine told, her that Joseph was already gone.

 Darren, Keith were still there, and also her likeness was still there as well. The next morning Justin arrived at the main house. Victor greeted him at the door, and showed him to his room. Where he freshened up, after his drive to Carington Point. Victor took Justin to the attic, to see where they were going to have the siance. Downstairs Edward and Rachel, were talking about what they were doing in the attic. Daniella heard what they were talking about, she ran to the attic. She told them that the ghosts were not bad, and to leave them alone! Their my friends and they are nonthreatening!

Charles came up to see what all the noise was about. They want to get rid of my friends, and I wont let them! Daniella and her dog left the attic, she was crying. She was yelling get out of here and leave them alone! Victor if you do this, I will always hate you! You know that Keith is not a bad ghost you've talked to him. Victor came down to talk to her, I don't want them to leave, if they are nonthreatening. But if they are bad I don't want them around you or your dog. All the siance is for is to have Justin see for himself, whether we should let them stay; or make them leave for good. You will see tonight that they are good, and then you can leave them alone! Justin asked, how many are there? Daniella told him there are four, two men, one woman and a boy. Edward and Rachel came up to see what was going on in the attic. Justin told them that the attic was dark enough to go ahead with the siance. And not to wait until nightfall. A voice told Daniella that one of the ghosts was gone. Now there were only three left, and that they will not come out until it is dark. She told them that they have to wait until midnight.

So they all left the attic, except Daniella and her dog. I will not let them get rid of you, I promise. Daniella and Katie left the attic and went to the den. Daniella locked the door she called, Katherine, Patricia, and Nicole. And asked them to come to the main house before midnight. Nicole told her that she could get Carol to cover for her at the pub for closing. Guinevere's spirit was restless, so she went to the caretakers house. To see her name sake and her sister she was not alone. Guinevere was followed by Darren and Keith, they went to ask for their help. We have lived in that house for hundreds of years we don't want to leave! Christine and Guin said, they would do their best to help.

Nicole called Carol and told her that she was sick, and that she was staying home for the day. Then she met Katherine and Patricia at the old grave yard. Then they went to the empty grounds keepers house. The three of them mixed a protection spell potion. To protect the spirits from being vanquished. As night fell the spirits returned to their home. Guin and Christine went to the graveyard. Where they met with the three witches. They went to the main house together. Daniella and her dog were waiting for them outside. They all began to chant in a language she did not understand. The women were also using the potion to bind the spell. When midnight fell upon the house every one came to the attic. To start the ceremony, Justin lit the candles and drew a pentagram on the floor. They all sat around the table holding hands. The five witches and Daniella came into the attic. Justin asked what they were there for? We are here to stop you, from making them leave their home! The spirits appeared, we are not going to hurt anyone, we want to live in peace. We are Daniella's friends, we want to coexist in peace, so please let us be and leave the attic now. Justin asked everyone to leave the attic except Victor. So everyone else that lived in the household left the attic. Victor, Daniella, Katie, the five women and the spirits stayed. Justin asked Victor who the five women were? Charles came back to the attic, and said one of them is my girlfriend. And one of them is Victor's girlfriend, Nicole waits tables at the Blue Moon Pub. We don't know who the other two are. Finally Guin spoke, I am Guinevere and this is my sister Christine. We are the grandchildren of one of the spirits standing before you. We are witches and we placed a binding spell on the house, To keep you from relieving this house of our family! We will stop at nothing to keep them here. Now that you have seen that they are nonthreatening please leave them be! Do as they asked leave now! Guin began to get very angered, she told Daniella to take her pet and leave. She told her that the men would not be hurt. She left but she was worried, that something bad was going to happen so she stayed close by.

    Guin asked him again to leave, when he did not. She asked Katherine and Patricia to take Charles and Victor and go! The four of them left, then she told Nicole to leave as well; so she did. That left Justin the three ghosts and the two sisters. We want you to leave this house now! Or we will make you leave forever! Guin levitated him off the floor, turned him to ward the stairs. She was going to throw him down the stairs. When her sister stopped her, put him down "Guin please. Just let him go don't hurt him, that's not what we came for!" Her wrath was stronger then her sister knew. She looked at Christine's face, she saw the anxious look in her eyes; the look of a sisters love and pain.

Guin put him down, Justin ran down the stairs as fast as he could. The two women vanished leaving nothing but a gray smoke behind them. Justin went to the room that Victor said he could use while he was there. He packed up his suitcase, Victor entered the room. Justin I didn't ask you, to come here to get rid of them at any cost. Daniella said, she would do anything to keep them here. I'm leaving because Guin told me to, I'm not leaving town, I'll be staying at the gatehouse with Charles.

He left with Charles, Guinevere and Christine were on their way home not saying a word to each other. Meanwhile Adrian was on the prowl for a victim. When he saw a young woman walking her dog all alone. A strange and eerie mist suddenly surrounded her and her dog. The dog growled fiercely at the mist, he knew someone or something was there. But he could see nothing at all.

The woman asked her dog what was wrong? All of a sudden her feet, were lifted off the ground; and when she came down. She was lying on her back, there was a man standing over; her he did not say a word. He slashed his wrist and made her drink. Adrian didn't kill her dog, he entranced him instead. The woman stood up, and asked him who and what he was? I'm Adrian and I am a vampire. What's your name? My name is Grace and this is my dog Spike. Adrian, Grace and her dog disappeared into a dense mist. Armand came upon the place where, Adrian and his latest victim had just left. Armand had a feeling that he was not alone. Bernadette, I know you are here Adrian is gone;

you can show yourself. She did not uncloak herself, she told him; with her thoughts that it was good to see him. Then she left, he was alone again. But not for long, Armand sensed that there was someone coming. It a woman and some kind of beast. Christine recognized his scent and removed her hood. Where is Guin? She is here with me. Show yourself, Guin Adrian is gone I'm here alone. Guin had Christine remove her cloak. Armand could not believe his eyes. Before him stood a large black winged wolf. For some reason she did not drink the wolfbane tea tonight.

Christine put the cloak over her sisters back, because someone was coming. Bernadette was heading home from her nightly hunt, as she came passed; she removed her hood. To greet her old friends, "someone else is coming! We need to leave now!" Armand told them, that he had no were to go and that he stayed where; ever he felt safe. Guin and her sister told him that he could stay with them.

They were all going in the same direction, any way so they all left togther. Guinevere told her sister and Armand, to get on her back. And to put the cloak over them, then flew back to the house. I transformed into Corina and flew home. When I reached the house, Joseph was waiting for me, if looks could kill I would be dead. "You bitch you lied to me, you're not a spirit like me at all you are a vampire!" I felt terrible, "Joseph let me explain please!" "Oh I will, I have all the time in the world. After all I'm already dead, so I'm not going anywhere. Who did this to you? And when did it happen?" "Adrian is the one whom, made me what I am; while you were away. Buying textiles for your plant. I was out taking a walk, when I ran into Adrian. After he turned me, he took me to his house. He would not let me leave, unless he came with me. My powers grew very fast too fast, for him to keep track of me. One night we were on a hunt, while he was with his prey; I took advantage of it. I turned into a crow and flew away, when I came back you were still at sea." Joseph looked at her and said, "when I came back they told me that you had died. They did not tell me how or from what! Just that it was a sudden death. Now I know that the coffin next to mine is empty." "The only one that knew that I was not dead is Willa. She was the one that told me that you killed yourself." "I did not jump I was pushed, off the cliff by someone. I could not see them but I knew they were there." "Adrian told me, that he would; do anything he could to keep me for himself." "So he is the one who killed you! I am so sorry Joseph please forgive me." "Why are you sorry, there is nothing to forgive you for this wasn't your fault." "I told you I'm not going anywhere. I'm staying right here with you." I smiled at him, which is something, I had not done in years. Joseph smiled at me and said, "I would have killed him before all of this had happen." Willa knocked on the door, I answered it and asked her what was wrong? Willa told me that nothing was wrong, she told me that Albert called and asked her out for the evening. I told her to go and have fun, please be very careful. I will be as careful as I was before I promise. Willa told me that she had placed fresh blood in a refrigerator in my closet. Because she knew I really did not like killing anything at all. I thanked Willa for her kindness, I do not know what I would do with out her. She has been my only friend all these years. Willa left a note for me, it read, I had a false wall placed in the back of your closet.

When you want to open it, just lightly push on the left side; of the wall and it will open. I did just that and behind it was the fridge. I took a pint of fresh blood out and drank it, then I closed the false wall. I turned to Joseph, and said nothing. He just looked at me with great sadness in his eyes.

"Joseph I know you can not become a human again. So I want to die and become a spirit like you."

Over at the main house, Edward had just come back from the textile mill and the boat dock. He went to check up on the workers, and the shipments. Rachel was in the den, working on the companies books. Edward sat next to her, to go over the books. When they were done, he got up to leave the den; Rachel told him. That she had hired a cook/maid and that she had a daughter the same age as Daniella. "What's the woman's name"? "Her name is Clementine and her daughter's name is

Rebecca." In the morning, bright and early there was a knock on the door. Rachel answered, it and there stood their new help. She took them to their rooms to put their bags away. Daniella came down and went in the kitchen. For something to eat, she saw a girl sitting at the table reading a book. Daniella went over and asked the girl what her name was? The girl told that her name is Rebecca, she asked her what's yours? My name is Daniella, and this is my dog Katie. Clementine came into the room and said, I see you to have met. Why don't the two of you go out and play in the back. "While I cook breakfast, I will call you when it's done." The two of them went out back to play with each other and Daniella's dog. Charles and Justin went to the main house. Victor was in the drawing room, with Edward and Rachel having coffee; and reading the paper. Clementine called everyone to the table. This the first time in years that everyone sat at the table together.

Daniella told her father that she, wanted Rebecca and her mother; to eat with them. Or she was going to eat with them in the kitchen. He said that would be fine with him. At the old house Willa was sitting all alone eating. When suddenly there was a knock at the door, she went to answer it. Albert was standing there with flowers in his hand. I came to see if you would like someone to eat with. She let him in and said, I made enough for two, please come join me. As they sat down to eat, Bella Noir came down stairs. Albert said, I did not know that you had a cat. She's cute, he read her tag Bella Noir what does that mean? She said, beautiful darkness, while they were having their coffee by the fireplace. Albert's radio phone went off, the Sheriff told him to come back; to the office A.S.A.P, He thanked her for the meal and left. After he left I changed., from a cat to myself. He seems nice, you like him I can tell. I'm glad you have found someone. It will make my, decision much easier to make. What do you mean by that? I have decided to find someone to kill me. So that I can be with Joseph, and now that you have found someone to spend time with. You will not miss me as much, we rarely see each other anyway. I know that you are not happy Willa. I also know that you are lonely, or you were until now. Joseph and I

will still be here for you when you need us. Bernadette are you sure this is what you want? That is the first time you have, ever called me by my name. And yes this is what I want. I hate my life such as it is, I miss the
    sunlight, the smell of flowers and the sound of birds. I will find a way to leave you Bella Noir or find a cat that looks just like her. I'm going out to find someone to do the deed. I will miss you old friend very much. I'll be here in spirit form. I know Willa that you can see and talk to spirits so you wont be lonely. You can call on us and we will appear. When nightfall came I went out, to look for someone to help me. Leave behind the life I hated most of all. I came upon Armand, Christine and Guinevere. I showed myself, Guin asked me what was wrong? I told her that I wanted to die, and that I was looking for someone to kill me. They will not have to take my head, all they will have to do is stake me through the heart. Adrian and Grace suddenly appeared with Spike, Adrian looked at me, and said you want to die!? I will not let that happen you belong to me! I will not let anyone kill one of my wives ever! I do not belong to you, I'm Joseph's wife! I'm not yours not now or ever! Adrian you have no hold over me! You really talk big, when your friends and my brother; are around Bernadette! I'm much stronger than you are, you vanish and float throw people; like rag dolls. And you can read minds, but you can't bite people with out pain. You can't turn into an animal of any kind. And you can? You forget Adrian, I'm also a witch, my powers are even stronger then yours! Yet I turned you into what I am! Because you killed me when you killed Joseph! I was wondering when you were going to come to me about that! Guinevere and Christine, did not drink their tea that night. Because Willa called them with her thoughts, and told them about Bernadette. Needing help if she should run into Adrian. Not knowing that they were there even before I came. I was glad they were there to help. They turned into winged lycans, standing one on each side of me.
    Armand stood behind me, so I was protected on all sides. All of a sudden, Adrian sensed that the woods were full of power, he had never felt before. When Adrian looked around, he saw Willa, Katherine and

Patricia. He even saw Joseph's spirit, I began to laugh. Your out numbered Adrian, you only have Grace and Spike with you. Unless you have someone, else with you we don't know about. No I don't you win this time! I didn't win anything, it's just that I have more friends; then you do that's all. Adrian, Grace and Spike left, I thanked everyone for all of their support. Katherine and Patricia left, the rest of us left as well. As we left, Adrian came back alone. He found a woman, sitting by a tree crying. He went over and asked her what was wrong? She said nothing at all, because she was mute. He helped her up, drank from her. When he was done, he turned her then they left. Just as the Sheriff and Albert came walking through. They had gotten a call about a fight in the woods. Shots being fired they found blood on the ground. They also found a body it was still warm. They called the doctor, to have him come and pick; up the body. When they found the person with, the gun he was drunk. I thought it was a mad dog it's foggy. I only heard it I couldn't see it. I didn't know it was a person. They took him back to the jailhouse.

I was outside of the gatehouse, I heard Justin and Charles talking. Someone told me, that there are vampires and werewolves around here is that true? Charles said yes, it is true why do you want to know? Because I would like to kill one. Why would you want to kill one? So they couldn't hurt anyone I love, or even a friend. Charles got up and left the room. Justin went outside for some air.

I showed myself to him. I said, I can give you what you want. And what's that? A vampire to kill, do you know where I can find one? You are talking to one, I will not harm you, I do not kill people.

Where do you get your blood? From a fridge in my room. Why do you want to die? Because I hate what I am, I want to be with my late husband. Did you kill him? No I did not someone else did.

When do you want me to kill you? Right now you only have to stake me in the heart. There's no need to take my head. Here take this stake and hammer. I will lay down right here. I thought that it was supposed to be done in daylight, when you are asleep. No it does not just do it please!

Justin got down on his knees, put the stake over her heart. Took the hammer, hitting it as hard as he could; blood spurted into the air. Shutting my eyes, I was gone. My spirit was looking down and smiling. I thanked him for releasing me, then my body vanished. Willa was crying, Adrian knew that I was gone, and he screamed out in pain. Because someone he had made died. Joseph and I were together at last. Guinevere and Christine took Willa home. Armand went along, as for the spirits of her departed friends we went with them. When Willa and the others got to the house, there was a cat laying on the sofa. That looked just like Bella Noir. That night Willa called Albert.

She told him that the woman she was caring for, had died of a heart attack in her sleep. Albert came and stayed in the guestroom he decided to move in with Willa. From then on neither one of them were alone. Guinevere and Christine, had made up their minds about being beasts of the night. We will go out and spread our wings, but we must not be seen by the naked eyes of other people. We must never take a life of a human nor beast, that is a vow we must keep.

Bernadette's Epitaph

I Bernadette wish to depart, from my eternal misery. For I grow weary of this life, that was chosen for me against my will though Willa the dear cares for me so. Though I value and cherish her loyalty and her friendship. I still feel lonely like, a part of me is missing. In my solitude, I contemplate my true purpose here. I have come to my final decision, I want to leave this life behind. I have lost everything, that had any true meaning to me. So as my final request, I desire more than anything. Is to reunite with my beloved departed Joseph. Then and only then I will be free. From the dark curse that binds me. And we can be once more. The way we were meant to be. I bid farewell.

Torment Thy Name is Bernadette

My life ended the night I became the daughter of darkness. Since then I haven't been the same. For I have lost everything, and everyone I held dearest to my heart. Now I am consumed by never ending darkness. That is now my miserable existence. Never to walk the light of day. Or feel any human emotion. To some it is a gift to be able to live forever. But in my eyes it is a curse I can't escape from. Except perhaps in death, so I can be with my beloved once more in the afterlife.

Williamina Adams Diary

*M*ost of my life I served as a watcher for a vampire named Bernadette. After a while she became more than a master. She became my one and only friend, where ever she went I went as well. We did not spend much time together, because when I was awake she was asleep. When I was asleep she was awake. And not in the house. I spent most of my time alone, reading or cleaning. Until I met Albert I was a very lonely woman.

Joseph's Diary

I was a textile merchant and I traveled a lot, my wife Bernadette and I didn't see each other most of the time. While I was away at sea, my wife was taken from me, by an evil vampire named Adrian. When I came home, I was told that she had died in her sleep. I went to Widower's Peak to kill myself, when I got there I changed my mind. I was about to turn back, when someone came behind me. And pushed me off the peak, I now know that someone was Adrian.

All My Love

All my love
I give to you
From the very
First day I saw
you I knew right
There and then
that you felt the
same way about
Me as I did for
you that very first
day we loved each
Other that way from
then till the day
We said I do and
until the day you
past away all my
Love I gave to you
and I give to you still
the love of my life
my late beloved
wife Bernadette

By Joseph Carington

Guinevere's Diary

*M*y name is Guinevere, I'm the oldest of two sisters, my sister and I are cursed. We have been since birth, she is the only constant person in my life. That has remained beside me since the deaths, of my husband Darren and our son Keith. In a way we are kindred spirits, not only by blood. We both share the curse, of becoming a werewolf. In order for us to stay our mortal forms, we must drink a special blend of tea. It is not a cure, but it hinders the transformation. I know this is not much of a life. But it is unfortunately for us, the only one she and I know. We cope with it the best we know how to.

Christine's Diary

My older sister and I were born with the curse, of becoming werewolves. A witch placed a spell on our mother. Before my sister and I were born, now in order not to turn. We have to drink wolf bane tea, when we do not want to turn. Into flying black wolves. I am not happy at all with this life, but I do not know anything else. But this miserable existence that was placed upon us.

Adrian's Diary

I am a vampire and not by choice either. To my victims I choose to say, I could give you a choice; to become what I am or not. But I choose not to, because I never had the choice. So why in the hell should I give one to you! You will get the dark gift whether you want it or not! Once I give it to you, your mine forever! And when I tire of you I may let you live, or I may kill you!

Armand's Diary

*L**iving in the shadow of my sadistic brother, I would consider myself an outcast. Unlike him I do not take pleasure, in tormenting others for my own amusement. I myself was more of a loner, for I was usually alone most of my life. Though we share the same blood, we are as different as night and day. I am a warlock and he is a vampire. However I never felt the need to reveal it. That I am a warlock, often if at all because I just wanted, to belong somewhere. I grew tired of being displaced, until Guinevere and Christine took me in out of the kindness of their hearts. For in truth it was rather lonely being me. Thanks to them I'm not lonely anymore.*

Victor's Diary

I have been Daniella's male nanny and tutor for ten years. I have always felt sorry for her. Because her father, has always been to busy to spend time with her. He is a single business man, everyone else in the house are much older than she is. The only friends she has are the ghosts, in the attic and her dog Katie. She did not have anyone else to play with. Until the cook/maid moved in with her daughter Rebecca.

Daniella's Diary

My name is Daniella and I can see and talk to ghosts. I have a very lonely childhood. Every one is much older then I am, my only friends are the ghosts in the attic. Of our house and my dog Katie, and for a while Keith one of the spirits. Was the only one close to my age, to play with. We were the only children that lived there. I was a very sad child, no believed me, they all thought I was nuts except Victor. I was really glad when Rebecca, moved in with us. I finally had a friend that was a live, I was not sad anymore.

Dark Dynasty
Part 2

The Soraier's Coven

We are the witches that live, in Caringnton Point; our story begins here. Many years ago on Hallows eve we were vanquished by a demon named Maladis! We turned him into a statue, and locked him away in a crypt. When we went to the graveyard, we came across that very same statue. Standing in front of the caretakers house, where Adrian lived. Willa was very angry, "what the hell is this doing here!?" "How in the hell did it get here!?" Nicole said, "we have to take it back, before midnight or he will come back to life!" Sara said, "let's take it back to the mausoleum; where we cast our spells and lock it up." The six of them vanished with the statue. When Adrian appeared with Grace, Spike and May; he was pissed! "Where is my statue of Maladis!?" Armand was standing in the shadows trying not to laugh, at his insane brother. He had his old friend Tomas with him, I told him that I knew where it was. They were heading toward the mausoleum to meet with the witches. When Christine and Guinevere, came up behind them; and asked what was wrong? Tomas told them that Adrian, had brought the statue of the evil demon. Maladis back with him from the past. "We must put him back before midnight approaches." "Or he will come back to life, when the full moon rises. Tonight is supposed to be the night of the crimson moon. The black rose of death, comes into full bloom tonight at midnight. The scent alone will awaken him. We need to take him back to the crypt, that we put him in." Tomas said, "we need the metal coffin, we locked him in before we can put him back in the crypt." Carol said, "Adrian has it and he wont give it up with out a fight." Willa said, "I have one at the house, we can go and get it and take it there." Sara told them, that she could do it; without even leaving the mausoleum. What they didn't know was that, May was watching them. She went back to Adrian, and signed to him where the statue was being kept. "Damn it! I wanted to bring him back to life!" Bernadette drifted in and started to laugh. "What's so damn funny! If I may ask?!" "You are being out witted by a coven of witches." "I'll get him back before midnight." "Not if I can help it you wont!" "What in the hell can you do your a ghost!?" "I am also a witch I still have my powers. They will be able to take, him to where he was before if I help them." Then Adrian turned to Grace and asked her, "why there was not anyone; standing guard like I told them to!" Bernadette had already left, she was on her way; to help them take the statue back. When she got there it was to late! What the hell happened?! The room that we placed, him in was not as strong as the one he was in before. Where is he?! He might of headed back to Adrian's! Maladis will not be as strong here. As he was back in our time, we should be able to vanquish him once and for all. Because he is out of his element here. Tomas looked at Bernadette, with sadness in his eyes. I'm much happier this way. I'm with Joseph again and that's the way it should be. We need to find Maladis, I know that he will be heading to Adrian's. The whole coven headed to the graveyard to confront Maladis face to face. When they got there, Adrian was waiting for them with his whole clan. We know you brought him here. We will find him, and send him back to hell; where he came from. Maladis show yourself now! The air filled with a thick smoke, as a large beast appeared before them. Fire balls were thrown, and lightning bolts went flying then thunder clapped. Maladis was losing his strength. The witches surrounded him chanting. Maladis you demonic demon, depart from here now! And go back to the dark fiery depths of hell! Where you belong never to return! Maladis vanished from sight, never to be seen again. Adrian was furious so much so, that any on looker. That came through the woods, to see what was going on would become his prey. The coven did everything they could to stop him! Finally the only thing they could do, was to vanquish Adrian as well. With a heavy heart Armand, helped, them vanquish his own brother. Knowing that one day he may regret it. For now Caringnton Point, would only have to deal with is witches, ghosts and werewolves. As for the vampires they had Armand and Christine to guide them. They taught them to live off the blood of small animals. Or go to the blood bank for their blood. In order to survive, that way no more innocent people will have to die or suffer a cruel non death.

Dark Dynasty
Part 3

The Spectral Realm

After the witches and warlocks vanquished Maladis and Adrian, the town went back to as normal as it could. Everyone was getting ready for the fall, festival. Even the spirits were gearing up, for a party of their own. The witches were brewing up something special. The werewolves, were planning on having a howling good time. The spirits they liked this holiday most of all. This was the time of year. Where they could have all of the fun they wanted to. As long as they were not to vicious or violent about it. They did not want to be vanquished or banished. They would spend a lot of their time in the graveyard. Scaring the people, that went to visit the graves. Or haunting old or abandoned houses and churches. Bernadette and Joseph, were not going to join the others. In their childish pranks, they were going to stay at home. And spend their time, together with their pets. As if they were still a living couple. They felt that they were to old to play tricks on people. Willa knew that Albert, had to work but she didn't seem to mind. In her spare time she would read or play with her cats. Or she would go to the old house, to spend time with Bernadette and Joseph. The only spirits in the house that, went out to haunt, were Rick and Keith. The two youngest ghosts in the house. Rick was a spirit that Keith, met in the graveyard. He was an orphan that he brought home with him. He was lonely, after they left the main house. He no longer had Daniella to play with. Because she stopped coming to the attic to visit him. When she met Rebecca, he felt left out. Keith and Rick went to the main house, to try and scare the girls. Which they didn't at all, the girls were glad to see them. They all went to the attic to play. Daniella and Rebecca took their dogs with them. Meanwhile Justin went out looking for, demons, vampires, werewolves and ghosts. He also knew that he would find a witch or warlock as well. Because Halloween was, just around the corner. Witches liked Hallows eve the night of the black Sabbath, most of all. The spirits liked it all because, they liked the trick or treat pranks. These hauntingly fun pranks, include rattling changes, moving and flying objects. Lights flickering on and off, weird noises, fading in and out, going through walls and doors. Last but not least, flipping pages, and leaving messages on mirrors and window. Slamming doors, opening and closing drawers, and rustling curtains. Father Mc Foley, had many visits to his parish; when the fall festival came around. People would come to him, asking him to help them banish the spirits from their homes. Dr. Whitmore would have people, coming and telling him; that they thought they were going mad. Because of the sounds that they heard, and the things that they saw. In their homes and on the street, or in the graveyard. He would tell them not to drink anymore, go home and sleep it off. As for the priest, he smears their house with incense; then say a few prayers. Everything will be alright now, they should be fine the spirits have moved onto a new place.

Dark Dynasty
Part 4

The Lycon's Lair

Guinevere made sure that they, had a plentiful supply of wolf bane tea on hand. Christine made sure that they kept, their cloaking capes nearby as well. Tomas and Armand went everywhere they went. Armand was the only one, in the house that was not a werewolf. Tomas was the only one, that wasn't into witchcraft. Three of them went out at night, to hunt small animals. The four of them would help those in need. They never attacked a person, with out probable cause. They knew that Justin was on the hunt for werewolves and vampires. And anything unnatural that he could find. They did their best to remain hidden. The three werewolves liked to spread their wings every now and then. Armand once again felt out of place. He asked Christine, to bite of scratch him. So he as well could become a werewolf. She said no, so he asked Tomas to do it. He asked him, are you sure, that this is what you really want? Armand said yes, I'm sure. Tomas did what he was asked to do. With in 24 hours, Armand was no longer just a warlock. He was also anew born werewolf. That very night the four of them, went out for a cloaked flight. Armand saw the world through new eyes. While they were on their nightly flight. Justin knew that they were out there some where. Along with all of other inhuman and non mammals, of the night. He went to the Blue Moon where he met, a fellow hunter Gabrielle. Justin and Gabrielle, went to the graveyard.

Where they found the vampires lair. It was the perfect, time of day. To find and kill most of Adrian's followers. Justin slayed Grace and May, she slayed a few as well. They could hear Adrian's furious demonic screams from hell! As they killed some of his most faithful followers. Or as he called them his fallen dark angels of the night. Spike was howling, Armand told him that he heard him too. As they were flying, the night skies. They noticed a young woman in distress. They went down to help her, they did not let her see them. They through her attackers around, like rag dolls. Their clothes were all ripped up, and they had scratches all over them. Which meant that they also, will become werewolves as well. The men were unconscious, as was the woman. When she came to, there were four people; standing over her. And a dog sitting next to her. Are you all right miss? I'm fine now thank you, for helping me. You are welcome miss. Tomas helped her to her feet. Armand made sure that the mens scratches were not visible. When they came to the were tied up. Before anyone else saw, the four of them they cloaked their selves and vanished off into the night. After they left, Justin and Gabrielle found the men. Tied up before they could become, fully turned werewolves; they killed them. It was in deed a good nights hunt for them both. This was the first time that Justin and Gabrielle had ever gone on a hunt together. This would not be the only time that they would hunt as a team.

Maladis's Diary
October 28, 1918

My name is Marcus Caringnton, I am a felleopeer My tale begins in the early 1800s, my mother was cursed by a witch. The witch told her that all of her children would be fellow peer She did not believe her, she thought that it was an old wives tale. Until I was born, with hair on my face, that got worse when the moon was full. She sent me to live with the, gypsies. That's where I was given the name Maladis. They locked me in a cage, and fed me table scraps; like I was an animal. They whipped me when I was bad. After years of torture and a abuse. I grew to be cruel and angry. Everyone thought I was a monster. Or a foul demon because of my appearance. Which fueled my anger further! They considered me a threat, so to make sure I wouldn't harm anyone. They placed me in an breathable metal coffin, then they locked me up in a crypt. Far from where I was born.

The Death Rose

The blood red moon
Shines down on the
black rose of death
Some call it the
midnight rose or
dark beauty but
I call it the death
rose. Because anyone
who receives one as a
gift. Dies and if the
black rose is kissed, by
the light of the blood
red moon. Their death
will be swift and bloody
So beware of anyone
baring a black rose
Kissed by the blood
red moon as a gift.
Because that black rose
kissed by the blood red
moon shine is the rose
of death

We Are Not Alone

The sun rises the sun sets we are born we live, and we die. We go through life looking for a perfect mate. Never finding him or her thinking that, we are to live or die alone. But if we open our minds and our eyes we will find out. That we are never alone we have a whole, entourage following us. Where ever we go we can't see or hear them, but we know they are out there. We are forever looking for our soul mate someone whom we are to live out our life with. We don't have to look far, because he or she Or what ever we wish to call the Great Spirit. That gave us the right to be here. That is the one we need, we who think we are alone. Are wrong we have our guardian angels, and the spirits of our ancestors. And departed loved ones with us. Every day we have our family and friends that spend time with us in person. And on the phone, we have our pets. So why do we feel the need to keep looking, for our perfect mate. When we have everything we need right in front of us. Our pet is our best friend. The Great Spirit or Mother Nature may very well be our perfect soul mate
For we are not Alone

Dark Dynasty
Part 5

Screams From Hell

"I hate you Adrian!" "This is all your doing, I would not be here; if it were not for you! You should of just left me where I was!" "Well that's gratitude for you! I helped you get out of the hell, you were in and now you are free; you should be thanking me." Maladis looked, at him with fire in his eyes and in his heart. You are a sadistic ass, how in the hell am I free! When we are in hell it's self! Adrian this is where you should be. I do not belong here. You kill for the thrill of it, and I kill for survival." "I also take women for my brides, that have no one to take care of them." "Those women had no choice, and some of them did have someone to take care of them. You killed them to get to their women. And you can't tell me that they really like the taste of blood. Or killing people for sport either. And not being able to have, a child with the one they really love. I really do not believe that they wanted to be blood sucking vampires like you either." "I did not want to be a vampire! Elzar did this to me and I hate him for it!" "I did not want this either, I was born this way. The gypsy witches did this to me, by putting a spell on my mother when she was pregnant." "Marcus we should be trying to find a way out of here." He just looked at Adrian and said, "you are right. Adrian you are also a warlock, can't you use your powers to get us out of here?" "I am but my powers will not work down here. And they are not as strong, as they were before I became a vampire." "Will your maker help you if you call him for help?" "He would but, I will not ask him for anything at all ever." "We might be able to get him trapped down here if he comes." "Marcus I hear digging above our heads. I think that we are just below a grave yard. A grave is six feet deep, if we can find a high spot we might be able to get out of here." "How about these rocks, here right below the grave." "It's still not high enough." "Here Adrian get on my shoulders; and dig with your hands." "I can see the moon light." Adrian climbed out and then he helped Marcus out. They headed to the caretakers house in the grave yard. Where they cleaned up and changed. Adrian went to check up on what was left of his many wives. They were all glad to see him, or as glad as undead women could be that is. While Adrian was with his many wives, Marcus took a cloaking cape and left. He was hoping that he could find someone, to help him become a normal human. While he was walking he came across an old house, he went in to get out of the cold. He heard voices but he did not see anyone at all. All of a sudden he saw a woman's spirit standing in front of him. It was Bernadette, she asked him how he got in? And who he was? "My name is Marcus Carington, and the door was unlocked and that's how I got in." "Why are you here?" "I am here to ask you for help. Why did you ask me all of that, when you know who I am. Because you were one of them that put me in that foul place that I was in. I am not the one that you need to be worried about Adrian is also out." "I do not have to worry about him, I am all ready dead." "Then you can't help me, I do not want to remain like this anymore. I want to be normal, I am tired of people running away, from me when they see me." Marcus stared to cry, "I can help you. Stay here I will be right back." When she came back she brought the rest of her coven with her. She told them that he was no longer a threat, and that he wanted to a normal immortal man. They formed a circle around him and began to chant. Marcus fell to the floor, when he came to his feet he felt very strange. He went to a mirror and looked at himself. He could not believe what he saw, he no longer looked like a beast. He looked like a normal young man. He looked, at everyone and said thank you. Bernadette asked, him where he was going to stay? He said, I do not know, I really have no where to stay. Tomas said, "you can stay, with us in the caretakers house." Before they all left they were trying to come up with a way to get rid of Adrian. Marcus told them that he wanted to get revenge against Elzar. "Does anyone know where he is?" "Tomas said, I know where he is," "but I'm not going to go back, to that time period ever again.""Then we will have to find away to bring him to us then." Carol asked, how do we do that? Willa said, we will use Adrian to bring him to us."Armand said, we make Elzar think that Adrian needs his help. My brother is his favorite vampire son. If he thinks that he needs help he will come to his aide. If we get rid of Elzar we will not have to kill my brother. Because he will no longer be a vampire, he will only be a warlock." Bernadette left before anyone knew she was gone. She went to see Adrian, and ask him to help them get rid of his maker. So that he could be free of the life he hated the most. He told her that he would be willing to help, get rid of him. Bernadette, took him to the old house, and put him in her room. Then she went to get Justin and Gabrielle, at Katherine's old flat. She brought them to the house. Then she went to her room, she told Adrian that she was going to pour water over his head. He asked, her if it was holy water? She told, him no it is not holy water. Armand does not want you to die. He wants his brother back that he misses, the one that took care of him when your parents died. She was about to pour the water over his head, when all of a sudden the room; filled with a thick black smoke. And there stood the one that made him, into the monster that he had become. You will not kill him while I'm here! Joesph said, you can not kill my wife because she is all ready dead. Bernadette poured the holy water on Elzar. Justin and Gabrielle came into the room, and shot an arrow through his black heart. He vanished into thin air and all that was left was a thick black smoke. Adrian was laying on the bed, when he came to he felt weak. He asked for a glass of water. Armand handed him the glass and helped him to his feet. He gave his brother a hug, he thanked them; for what they did for him and his brother. As everyone was leaving the house, Adrian thanked Bernadette for all of her help. As for all of the women that he had turned into vampires, they all became human again. The people of Carington Point still however had the werewolves to worry about. Because as long as Taltazer is still alive there will be the werewolves to deal with. Guinevere and Christine went to the other witches to ask them for their help to get rid of Talatazer. They wanted them to summons him so that they too could become as normal as an immortal person can be. So they did just that, and when he appeared; Justin and Gabrielle shot a silver arrow right through his chest. And then they set him on fire. All of those that were werewolves, became what they once were before. Either normal humans or immortal beings. Willa turned Albert into an immortal so that she would not be all alone. As for all of the other people in Carington Point, they were able to go back to life as they know it. The other Carington's did the same they went back to the same boring and mundane life style. The witches stayed in town to help when ever they could. All those that were once either vampires or werewolves. For the first time in years; people were going outside to in joy the sun light. That they have not seen in years. When night time came everyone in town, went out side with out being afraid. Or maybe they should not become, to accustomed to the calm for it may not remain that way for long.

Marcus's Diary

*A*fter years of being abandoned, tortured and neglected. As a punishment for being the way I once was. I never had a chance, to know what it was like to be a human. And to be able to live a normal life. Now for the first time I have that chance. Not to be labeled a monster, or kept locked away like a freak. It's a foreign feeling to me. For I am finally free, from the hell that once was my existence; for to long.

Adrian's Diary

I was a vampire most of my live, living off other peoples blood to survive. Ever so often I would claim a bride, or an unwilling victim. I had grown accustomed to my existence. It was all I knew for many years until now, it's irony really. Being a new warlock, not having to drink blood or living in the darkness anymore. In away I miss my former self. It was part of who I was, and on the other hand I'm grateful. To finally live a normal life I never had a chance to live.

Damius's Diary

My name is Damius I am Maladis's older brother I too am a beast by birth. I am not as forgiving as he is, I've been killing off as many of those damned gypsies as I can. I will not rest till every last one of them, that did this to us is dead. My brother's been reborn as a human, and is starting over. In a way I envy him for I'm still a demon, for all time! Forever being hunted down wherever I go. So I guess it's kill or be killed.

Dark Dynasty
Part 6

Thou Wrath of Damius

Marcus finally had the displeasure, of meeting his older brother for the first time. He was very glad that he did not have his girlfriend Nicole with him. Damius, looked at him with envy in his eye. He came over to Marcus and said, nice to finally meet you bro. Who are you? Why did you call me that? I have no brothers or sisters that I know of anyway. Damius looked at him and said, we have two sisters, I am the oldest; My name is Damius. Where are our sisters? What are their names? Their names are, Angaline and Linette. They live with me, in a house out side of town. Why are you here? I came from our time, to see if any of the witches; that cast the spell on our mother live here in this time. Marcus asked him, what will you do when you find them? I will kill them! That will not bring back our parents. No but maybe it mite, lift the curse from the rest of our family. I know that you will not help me. Now that you are no longer one of us. No I will not help you kill for revenge. I hope for your sake that you will not get in my way then! I would hate to kill my only brother! You don't know where I can find any of them do you!? No I do not! Would you tell me if you do know?! No I would not! Marcus walked off not looking back. He knew that his brother was watching him. His sisters did not want any part in killing of the witches ether. Damius was on his own when it came to that. Marcus could read his brothers mind, he knew that, he had all ready torched and killed six of them. He only had six more to kill. Marcus knew that his brother could not read minds. Because he was thinking, I hope that none of my new friends; have any thing to do with the curse. That was placed on their mother, he was also hoping that none of them had any gypsy blood running through the vanes, or in their family history. He had taken one of Nicole's cloaking capes with him. He was glad that he did. Because he was able to get home with out his brother following him. When he got home he asked Nicole, if she had any gypsy blood in her family? She asked, why did you ask me that? Because my my brother and sisters are here from from the past. He is here to kill the last six witches from the coven that placed the spell on our mother. That made all of her children into fisloepeers. What does that mean? It means lion like beasts. You mean like you were before? Yes and I'm glad that I am not on anymore. I really hope that for their sake, that none of the other witches have gypsy blood in their families ether. Do you know if your sisters are helping him? No they are not, I can read minds. They want nothing to do with killing anyone. Do you know where they are? Damius told me that they are staying with him. In a house just outside of town. We should find away to bring your sisters here. Then we can change them the way we changed you. To prove that not all witches are evil. And to prove to him that we, did not have anything; to do with the curse that was placed on your mother. What are we going to do about my brother? We will have to have the demon hunters kill him. If that is what we must do, then we will do it. I know that you will not want any part, in it because he is your brother. We will call upon Justin and Gabrielle to do it. Even though they were no longer able to turn into flying wolves, Guinevere and Christine. Still had the skill of flight because of their art of witch craft. They made a cloaked flight to the house, where Marcus's sisters were staying. They brought them back with them, and changed them into two beautiful young ladies. When Justin and Gabrielle got to the house Damius was gone, Justin said. He must have gone back to the past, to find the other six witches. We will wait here till he comes back. They were there for 48 hours, finally he came back. There was a fierce battle between Damius and the werewolves. When he could not fight anymore the two demon hunters shot him straight through his very black heart. With a sliver dipped arrow. Marcus and his sisters, were sad to see their brother die. But in the end they knew that it was the best thing to do. For the safety of every one in Caringnton Point. As for Bernadette and Joseph they are living a very happy live in the old house. Willa and Albert got married, Guin gave her away.

Dark Dynasty
Part7

Lusus Nalurae Domain

One dark foggy night a ship pulled into port carrying passengers. They had come to visit their families and friends for the holidays. Two of them were on the passenger list but not on any ones guest list. One of them was Charles's father. Whom everyone thought was lost at sea while fishing. And the other one was Daniella's mother Sofia. Charles's father Anthony and Daniella's mother Sofia, met in France. Anthony and Rachel had been apart 20 years. Because he was declared legally dead they were no longer married. Edward and Sofia were legally divorced. Sofia and Anthony got married in France. They were going to go to the main house, to visit the family they had not seen in years. They decided to stay at the inn, and go to the main house in the morning. There was one passenger that was not on the ships list. This one was someone that no one would want as a guest. He is just another skeleton in the family closet. That they would love to forget. His name is Luvyenne, he has a head like a hyena; and the body of a man. He is just one of many Caringnton's that are cursed. Luvyenne left the ship and made his way to the grave yard. Now that Adrian and his vampire brides were no longer living their. He assumed that the grounds keepers house was empty. He went in to make his self at home. And rest after his long trip at sea. He soon found that he was wrong. When he saw a large hideous figure, standing in the middle of the room. With his wings stretched out. "Who in the hell are you?!" "I am Luvyenne, I was hoping that this place was empty. So I could stay here while I was in town." Antonis said, "you can stay if you like, but I am not leaving!

"Fine then we will try not to, get in each others way then." Meanwhile Sofia and Anthony decided go to the Blue Moon to eat. Charles, Kathrine, Victor and Patricia, came in right after they did. Kathrine looked over at the other table. She noticed that the older man sitting at the table. Looked a lot like Charles. She looked at him and said, "Charles that man over there looks a lot like you. Is that your father?" "No it can't be my father is dead, he died at sea while fishing." The others at the table noticed it too. Charles said, "again no it can not be him my father is dead!" Anthony over heard what they said. Sofia told him to go over to the table. Anthony said, "they are right Charles I am your father." All Charles could say was, "you have a hell of a nerve, showing up here after all of these years! Who's that at the table with you!?" "That's my wife Sofia she is Edward's ex wife." "You married Daniella's mother! Oh that's going to go over really well! Talk about keeping it in the family! Did you have any children!?" "No we did not son." Sofia came over to the table. "Charles, I know that you are in shock and angry. But please try to keep your voice down. We should be able to talk like adults." Victor spoke up, "he does have a point. Why did both of you wait so long to come to see everyone? Are either one of you dying?" "No neither one of us is dying. I heard that my son was getting married. And I wanted to be here for that." Meanwhile back at the grounds keepers house at the grave yard. There was a lot of tension between Luvyenne and Antonis. "This place is not big enough for the both of us! One of us is going to have to leave! Antois said, it's not going to be me!" So he took Luvyenne to the old house next to the grave yard. "You can stay here for as long as you want. This will be your new home." The next day Sofia and Anthony went the main house. They were not welcomed with open arms. Edward took Sofia a side and asked her, "why in the hell are you here after all these years?" "I want to see our daughter. I did write to her and I sent her pictures of me. So she would remember what I look like." "I don't give a damn Sofia, she may not want to see you at all! It's bad enough that you show up after all of these years. Then you added insult to injury by marrying Rachel's ex husband! Or what we thought was her late husband!" "I'm not leaving with out seeing Daniella first." All of a sudden Daniella comes into the room with her dog, Rebecca and her dog. She looks at her mother and said, "hello mother long time no see." Then she looks at her father and says, "I'm going out to play now, I will see you when it is time to eat." Her father said, "that will be fine dear." Her mother looked at her and said, "Before you go I'm sorry that you dislike me so much. That you can't even hear my side of what really happened. Between me and your father, and why I left the way I did." "Daniella looked at her mother and said, "when I'm ready to hear your side of the story I will let you know. Until then I'm going out to play with my friend and our dogs. Please feel free to stay for dinner if you would like. I will tell the cook to set two more plates for the table." Rebecca asked, Daniella why she disliked her mother so much? "If you noticed my mother was not here when you got here. She has not been here since I was two years old". "I have been raised by my father ever since. Aunt Rachel and now Victor." Rebecca said, "I'm so sorry, I don't know what I would do with out my mother. I grew up with out a father. My father died when I was just a baby. So I never even got to know him. All I have is his picture that I keep by my bed. So that I can look at it before I go to sleep." The two girls and their dogs went out to play in the back yard. Meanwhile inside the house Rachel was having an argument with Anthony. When Sofia and Edward walked into the room. Sofia went over and stood by Anthony. Anthony said, "may be we should not have come here after all." Sofia said, "we are not leaving I want to get to know my daughter better. It is not my fault that I left the way I did. And you know it to Edward! You made me leave because you were afraid that I would become one of Adrian's victims. Or what he called his dark angel brides of the night. Well I heard that he is no longer a vampire and no longer a threat to anyone." "All right you can stay, you are right I can't make you leave. But the two of you will have to stay at the inn. If you do not have enough money to pay for the room I will pay for it for you." Daniella said, "no father now that the spirits, are no longer living in the attic; we can fix it up to look like a small apartment. And put a bathroom in it too." Her father said, "and how are we going to do that dear?" She looked at him and smiled then said, "witch craft that's how dad." So that night Daniella. Rebecca, Patricia and Kathrine, went to the attic and made it into a small but quaint apartment for two. Kathrine and Patricia used their witch craft to transform the attic. While Rebecca and Daniella put in the finishing touches. When they were done Daniella took Sofia and Anthony up stairs. To show them where they were going to stay while they were there. Back at the grave yard Antonis had decided to go out for his nightly flight. Meanwhile Luvyenne decided to go out and look around to see what his new homeland looked like. He was also looking for a new victim to turn into what he is. He ran into Adrian and his old friend Dominique. They were out for a nightly stroll. Adrian asked him, "who in the hell are you? And what in the hell are you?" He said, "I'm Luvyenne and I'm a beastly demon. How would you to like to look just like me!" Adrian started to laugh and then said, "I don't think so, you have met your match!" Then Adrian and Dominique used their combined powers to toss him like a rag doll. Luvyenne got up and ran off howling in pain. They decided to fly home, so they turned into two black; owls and headed home. Luvyenne went home pissed because he did not get to turn anyone that night. When Adrian and Dominique got back to the house. That Adrian moved into when he left the grounds keepers house. She asked him, "what in the hell was that thing that we encountered in the woods?" Adrian said, "It looked like it was half hyena and half man." Dominique said. "I'm so glad that we have the powers of witch craft on our side. Or that beast would of turned, both of us into the same hideous beast like him."

Adrian looked at her smiled and said, "I am glad you are here because I felt so lonely.

Even though I have Spike, he is a good friend for a dog that is. But it's not the same thing. Because he can't talk so its like having some one only not." Dominique smiled and said, "I'm glad to be here I missed you a lot." After his nightly flight Antonis headed home. He heard moaning coming from the house where Luvyenne was staying. He did not go over to see if he was all right. Because he knew that he must of met some one that was stronger then he was. And it was obvious to him that he did not get what he wanted. And that was to turn someone into the hideous beast that he is. The next day was the day of the double wedding. Between Charles and Kathrine, Victor and Patricia. Patricia's father Sean was going to give her away at the wedding.

Victor's father Shane was also going to be there. Patricia's father was also going to give Kathrine away because her father passed away. Her mother also had passed on. Almost everyone in the family was invited. That meant that the cursed ones, in the family were definitely not invited. Christine Guinevere, Tomas and Armand were sent an invitation to come to the wedding. Armand asked, if Adrian and Dominique could come as well? Edward said yes just to make Sofia mad. They also wanted to know if they could bring Marcus and Nicole. Rachel said that would be fine. Patricia also invited the waitress that work at the Blue Moon. Daniella went to the old house to talk, to Bernadette, Joseph and the other spirits. She told them that wedding would not be complete with out them there too. Bernadette said that they would be there. "But we will not let our self's be seen by any of the guests." She asked, if Willa and Albert could come? Daniella said, yes they can come as well. Victor asked, Justin and Gabrielle to come as well. The other guests on the list are, Sheriff Martin Mc Smith, Dr. Whitmore. And of course the one that's officiating over the ceremony Father Mc Foley. And last but not least the one cooking and serving the food Clementine the cook/maid and her daughter Rebecca. Clementine will be getting some help cooking, serving and cleaning up after the reception. After the ceremony Carol, Sara and Nicole will be helping her a long with her daughter Rebecca and Daniella. Everyone was in place waiting with great anticipation for the wedding to begin. Sofia and Anthony helped Rachel and Edward with the chairs the night before. Antonis never came out in the day time. But today he decided to do just that. He put on a cloaking cape and headed to the main house. He did not want to miss out on all of the fun. He also wanted to be there to protect his family from harm. Some how he knew that Luvyenne, might try to crash the wedding. And he was right he followed him to the main house. Luvyenne was heading straight for the back yard where everyone was waiting for Father Mc Foley to start the ceremony. Finally the music started to play. The young men were standing, in front of Father Mc Foley. The two young ladies were walking down the aisle. When all of a sudden they heard growling and howling in the front yard. Adrian, Armand and Tomas went to the front of the house to see what was going on. When they got around the corner. They found Antonis and Luvyenne fighting. The three of them were just, strong enough to stop the fighting. They knew that they did not want to hurt Antonis. They did what they could to make sure that the demon hunters would not kill him. Armand put a cloaking cape over Antonis's back. Justin came around the corner and killed Luvyenne. After everything was calm they resumed with the wedding. They all had a good time at the reception. After it was all over they went their separate ways. Only getting together for holidays and other family functions.

Luvyenne's Epitaph

My name was Adam Carington, I went to the Orient to pick up fine silks for the textile mill. On my travels I was bitten by a hyena, twenty four hours later. I was transformed into a hideous beast like demon. Half man half hyena the person I once was. Was gone forever! Adam no longer existed Luvyenne was born I became cruel and angry for what

I had become. Trying to turn anyone who crossed my path into a vicious demon. Much like I am now. I never asked for this but it was all I knew. I let it consume me like a disease. But in the end I met my timely demise, which sealed my fate!

Dark Dynasty
Part 8

Erelros Beastemmire

This is the final chapter of this story from the Carington family perspective. This part of the story is written by Bernadette (Stephanos) Carington. Oops my bad I for got to tell you from the very beginning that I am the sister to Edward and Rachel's late mother, Alisa Stephanos/Carington. I married her husbands first cousin Joseph Carington. Marcus had a good reason to be worried about the gypsy blood line. When his brother was killing off the witches that placed the curse. Because my half of the family is Greek and Italian gypsy. We did not how ever put the curse on my husbands side of the family. That curse was placed long before my sister and I were ever born. We never found out why it was placed on their family. We only know who placed the curse. Hopefully some day we will know why the curse was placed. And how to get rid of it once and for all. Until then all we can do is try to reverse the spell when ever we can. The curse usually is only placed on the men of the family. But some how it was passed down to Marcus's and Damius's two sisters. As you know from the beginning of this story my curse. Was inflicted upon me by that evil bastard Adrian. The once upon a time vampire, that is now just a warlock. The only other women in the family that had the curse was Guinevere and her sister Christine. There were only a few men that did not get in on this spell, they were few and far between. I am very glad that Willa is not a blood relative so she did not get hit with any of the cruel and vindictive curses. That the rest of us suffered. I am also very happy for her now that she is no longer alone. Now if Joseph and I should decide to leave this earthly plain. We will know that she will be well taken care of. As for the other spirits that lived, in the attic of the main house. And then moved to the old house. It's all up to them whether they move on or not. I told Willa that we would still come when ever she needs us for our help, or just to have company. Willa said to me, "Bernadette I will miss you a lot, because we have been together for such a long time." "I will be here with you all the time. All you have to do is look into the eyes of Bella Noir your cat, or the eyes of Corina your pet crow. And I will be right there looking back at you with a smile on my face. And listening to every word you say. All you will have to do is read the thoughts of your pets. To get my response to your thoughts or your words." Willa knew that she could also do that with her other cat Kama as well. Albert walked in while the two of them were talking. He went over to Willa and gave her a peck on her forehead. He then turned to Bernadette and said, "hello there it's good to sorta kinda see ya." Bernadette looked at him and said, "like wise Albert." Bernadette and Joseph said their good byes to Willa and Albert. And went back to the old house. Where the other spirits live and they are, Grandmother Guinevere, Darren, Keith and Rick. Over at the caretakers house, Armand, Tomas, Guinevere and Christine. Were sitting by the fireplace drinking wine and talking. When there was a tap on the door, it was Adrian, Dominique and their dog Spike. Armand opened the door and let them in. They all ate dinner together like one family. At the main house Edward came to a decision that he was going to, build another guest house. Next to the old one for Sofia and Anthony. He did not know that his sister had thought about it as well. Rachel all ready had men working on it. Edward had not walked around the grounds for some time now. The other guesthouse was all ready standing, and waiting for someone to move in. She was all ready moving everything out of the attic apartment, and over to the other guesthouse. Sofia was putting their things into it. By the end of that week the attic was once again empty. Edward decided to move into the attic for more privacy. Edward came across an old box of letters. That were written by their late father

Jonathan. When he was done moving, all of his things into the attic apartment. He sat by the fireplace and read them. He also found letters from their mother Alisa to their father. When he was done reading them. He took them downstairs. And let Rachel read them. Rachel asked where he found them? Edward told her that he found them in old boxes he found in the attic. Rachel said, "I did not know that Bernadette was our aunt on our mother side of the family. I also did not know that she was a damned vampire either!

How long have you known about that Edward?!" "I have known for quiet some time now. I did not tell you because. I didn't want you to be afraid to go for walks in the woods. That's why I would only let you go, for those walks in the daytime. Because I knew he would be out there somewhere waiting for his next victim." "And you thought that the next one might be me. Then when you got married and had Daniella. You thought it could end up being either Sofia or your daughter. So you sent your wife away, and hired Victor to watch over Daniella." "That's right I did not want her to lose her mother. The way we lost our mother and then our father shortly there after." Adrian always killed the men, that stood in his way of his female victims." Everyone that was at the caretakers house, was having a good time. They were laughing, drinking and playing games. Armand was glad to see the old Adrian that he remembered from their childhood. But in the back of his mind he kept thinking, I hope that this is not just an act for my benefit, and Dominique's. He may no longer be a vampire. But he is a very strong warlock, and one you do not want to make angry either. Dominique told Adrian that they should by heading home for the night. Even though they were not like other people they still every once in a while took short cat naps. To keep their strength up. Adrian smiled at her and said, "you are right dear we should be going home now." So they said their good nights to every one and left. They got into their carriage, with their dog and headed home. Marcus and Nicole were out for a late night walk. When they came upon the ugly beast Luvyenne. He wanted to know if they would like to join him. In his twisted life style. Nicole did her best to keep him as far away from them as she could. But her powers, were not strong enough to keep him back. And Marcus had none at all to help her out. All of a sudden here came Adrian and Dominique they got out of their carriage and helped them get rid of Luvyenne. Once again he ran off in pain howling all the way home. Adrian told them that they would give them a ride home if they would like. Marcus said, "that would be nice thank you, I'm glad that you two came by when you did." Dominique said, "you're welcome. I know that you would of helped her if you could of." Nicole said, "I will just have to teach you some spells to use. I will also ask the coven to help me give you the power to defend yourself better." When Luvyenne got to his house Antonis was standing right in front of him. He was laughing at him, "I see that you had another run in with Adrian." "It's not funny damn it! One of these days I will kill that smug bastard!" All that Antonis could say is, "good luck with that." Then he flew off for his nightly flight. While he was flying around he saw a beautiful young lady in need of help. So he came down to give a hand. She was trying to fight off a vampire. He made short work of him. He went off hurt and very pissed off! That he didn't get what he wanted.

Antonis asked, her if she was ok. She said, "I am fine now thank you for your help." He said, "you're welcome miss. Are you not afraid of me miss?" She said, "no should I be? You just saved my life for that I owe you a thank you. My name is Dora, what's your name?" "My name is Antonis."

"Well Antonis it was nice to meet you." "It was nice to meet you to Dora. "Before you go I really do not think that you should walk home alone. May I walk you back to where you live?" "I would really like that a lot. I do not live far from here." "Dora do you live alone?" "Yes I do way do you ask?"

"Because that vampire might come after you again. I also live alone, maybe we should stay in the same place. Together so that I can protect you better." "Where do you live?" "I live in the grounds keepers old house in the grave yard." "If we do stay in the same place, I think I rather it be my place. Because I really would not like to live in a grave yard."Very well then we shall go to my house. And get my things and we will take them to your house." While they were moving Antonis's belongings from one place to the other. They were being watched by two vampires. One of them was Athena and the other one was the one that let her get away. And that was Aineias he was very angry that she was saved by a werewolf. Athena was very angry with Aineias. Because he did not try harder to fight, for what he needed and wanted to survive. The two vampires left and went else where to find their next victims. Antonis and Dora finally made it to her house with what little he owned. Back at the main house Edward and Rachel, were very shocked! To find out that their fathers mother was the one that placed the family curse. On any man and some times women, in the family that married out side; the Greek/ Italian gypsy blood line, Edward said, "our grandmother Stephonia was not a very nice woman, you could say she was a real bitch." Rachel said, "shouldn't that be a real witch." He said, "isn't that like splitting hairs Rachel. I'm just glad that the curse passed us by all together." All she could say to that was, "me too Edward. Daniella, Rebecca and their pets came into the room. Daniella asked, her father what they were talking about? Edward told her it wasn't anything that she needed to worry about. Told the two of them to go get cleaned up for their nightly meal. Clementine called, them all to the table. Every one was there from Daniella's mother, stepfather, and both couples of newly weds. As time went by it became easier for all of them to be in the same room together. Clementine and Rebecca, were even asked to join the family. For their family meals, and other family gatherings. Charles asked, Edward about the family curse right at the dinner table. Edward said, "that it was not a good time to talk about it. With the young ones at the table." The two girls said we are old enough to here about it. Clementine told, them that she agreed with Edward. That they should come with her to the kitchen to eat their meal. So the others could talk, about grown up things that they were to young to hear. They reluctantly went with her to the kitchen with their drinks and plates. As they left the room they both said at the same time. We can't wait to grow up, so that we can stay in the room. When you are talking about stuff, that you think we are to young to hear. All they could do was laugh, because the girls reminded them; of the way it was for them when they were younger. After the laughing stopped, Edward asked, Charles what he wanted to know about the family curse. Charles said. That he wanted to know who placed the damn curse? And why they placed it on their family? Rachel told him, that it was his grandmother Stephonia that placed the curse on the family. And she did it because, she did not like it when someone; married out side our family blood line. Katherine said, "I thought that your family was Welsh?" Rachel said, "that's only on our fathers side, we are Greek/Italian gypsy on our mother's side." Charles said, "I'm glad that we are not part of the family that pissed her off." Edward said, "I'm glad too because I would not want to be a werewolf. Are what ever in the hell, that beast is that I saw. the other night in the woods. It scared the hell out of me. I hope that someone kills it soon before it kills someone we really care about." Charles said, "we can always go, and get Justin and Gabrielle to do it for us." Victor said, "that's true they are always, on the hunt for beasts and other creatures of the night to kill." Daniella came into the room and said, "why didn't any one tell me, about this cruel curse!? I have a curse of my own a can see and hear ghosts." Her father said, "dear we wanted to wait till you were older to tell about it." "Father I am 13 now I can handle anything you tell me. I thought I handled meeting my mother for the first time very well." Patricia said, "she is right you can't keep her in the dark about things like this. She would of found out some way or another. If she were our daughter, we would rather she found out what she would be up against. Before she meant one of the cursed ones face to face."

Dark Dynasty
Part 9

The Erebrus Bestemmire

My name is Antonis Stephanos, I am Bernadette and Alisa's cousin; on their fathers side of the family. I was a homosapien and now I'm a winged lycan. I was turned, by one of the quadrupad. Winged werewolves in Thebes(Greece). When I was just a child my mother, would lock me in my room until morning. Then she would let me come out when the sun came up. I was not aloud to play with the other children. Near our home because my mother did not want them to know my secret. So my parents home schooled me and I had to play with my siblings instead of the neighborhood children. We moved to Carington Point when I was 12 years old. I have lived here ever since then. Our house was burnt down while we were away on a family trip. My family moved back to either Thebes or Palermo(Italy) with out me. Because I was the only one that was cursed they left me behind. I was homeless moving from one empty house, to anther until I found one I could stay in. Now I am living with Dora in her home, I am happy now because I am no longer alone. I would be even happier if I were normal like she is. I for some reason can no longer return to my human form. Even when the sun comes up. The curse must have kicked in when I got older. Because when I was younger, I could always return to normal in the day time. Dora told me to go to the witches in my family. To ask them to do the same thing for me. That they did for Marcus and his two sisters. So Dora and I went to the family coven. To ask them to return me to my former self. They did what I asked them to do. They gave me back my life as a normal man. We thanked them all for helping me then we left. As for Luvyenne he was still a horrid angry beast. Going out every night trying. To find a new victim to either turn or kill. He really wanted to turn someone into what he was, because he in truth was very lonely. He wanted what all most every other beast had, that lived there got; and that was the life of being normal. He really did not want to die. He knew in his twisted and some, what cruel heart of his that could be his fate. He went out this time looking for some kind of help in stead of a victim. And who did he run into on his search for help but Adrian and Dominique. This time they were not alone they brought Justin and Gabrielle with them. Luvyenne told them that he wanted, to become a normal man. In stead of an ugly angry feared beast. They asked him, "why should we believe you? Every time we come across your path. You're always trying to turn some one or kill them." "Because that's all I have ever known. I have never known another way of life. But this one I am living now. I would like to have the life that you are living now." "How do we know that you will not continue to kill people even when you are normal? How can we trust you to be true to your word?" "Luvyenne said, "why is it that everyone else that was turned, into a normal human was trusted but me damn it!?" Dominique said, "that's why because you are to quick to anger. And that's why we will not help you with your request." Luvyenne said, "fine then kill me right here and now because I am tired of being alone. So rather than hunting me down. Why don't you just get over and done with! And kill me right here I wont try to stop any of you!" So Justin did as he asked and killed him right there and then. He shot an arrow right through his chest. He looked at Gabrielle and said, "we still have to deal, with the two vampires Athena and Aineias. And any other demonic demons. That are still out there just waiting for their next victim. To either turn into what they are, or to kill them just for their twisted pleasure." While they were talking Marcus, Nicole and Marcus's two sisters Linette and

Angeline. Came walking by on their nightly walk. Nicole knew right away that some one or something died there on that very spot that night. Nicole asked Justin, who died there that night? Gabrielle told her that they killed, the beast named Luvyenne there in that very spot. Linette asked her what the beast looked like? Justin told her that he had a face like a hyena and a body of a man. Linette looked at her sister and said, they just killed Adam Carington. Angeline said, ""I'm not sorry that they did he was very evil and cruel. And he no longer had any resemblance, to what he looked like when we were children way back when." Justin asked Angeline, how he was turned? She told him, that he was bitten by a hyena while he was in the Orient buying silk for the textile plant. Antonis was out on his nightly flight. He made sure that he cloaked himself so he would not be seen. He like all the others wanted to be freed, from the life that he despised the most. I do not like only going out at night and making sure that no one can see me or hear me unless they are in need of my help.

 He flew home with heavy despair in his heart. Antonis told Dora, that he wanted more than anything to be normal like her. Dora told him, to go to the witches for their help. She told him, that she too would love to go for walks with him in the day light. Dora went to Guinevere and Christine to asked them for their help. To turn Antonis into a human. They gave her a dagger made out of steel and dipped in wolf bane. They told her to have him stab himself, in the heart with it he will not die. He will return to his former self. She took the dagger back to the house and gave it to Antonis. He went into his room and did just what Dora told him to do. She heard him scream out in agony! She wanted to go to him, but she knew in her heart. That this was something he had to do on his own. So she waited out side because she could not stand the sound of his screams. When Dora came back in the house Antonis was sleeping. She could not stand to see all of the blood in the room. She went to Nicole and asked, her if she would use her powers to help her get rid of all of the blood in his room. When Antonis awoke the next morning he was a very handsome young man. He was so happy that he hugged Dora and gave her a kiss. For the first time in his life he went outside in the daylight. Dora joined him and they went for a nice long walk.

Dark Dynasty
Part 10

Athena & Aineias

Athena and Aineias were out on their nightly hunt. Looking for their next victim or victims. She liked to turn as many as she could in one night. Athena did not care if they were male or female.

The only ones she would not turn were children, elderly or weak people; that could not take care of their selves. Aineias was a lot like Bernadette, he did not like to take a life. Or turn anyone into the horrible monster that he was. Athena was a female version of Adrian. She would taunt and torment her victims before she turned them or killed them. Athena really liked toying with her male victims the most. She had Aineias turn the females because he had a much softer touch. He really hated the taste of blood, so much so, that he had his pet bat turn them for him. Athena knew what he was doing, but she did not care. She was still happy in her own twisted way. Because the more they turned the bigger her dark colony of vampires became. She knew in her black uncaring heart that Adrian would be very proud of her, if he were still the king of the night. For she was his first true fallen dark bride of the night. Or as she would call herself his one and only queen of the vampire domain. One night Aineias went out with his pet bat with out Athena. He went in search of the demon hunters. Aineias like Bernadette wanted to die.

He came across Justin and Gabrielle, he pleaded with them to kill him. He told them that he would do the same thing that she did. So he laid down on the ground and closed his eyes. Gabrielle knelt down next to him. And hit the stake as hard as she could with the hammer. The stake went straight through his chest and into his heart, the blood shot into the air. Just like Bernadette's body his also disappeared and so did his pet bat. Unlike Adrian, Athena was glad to be rid of him. Because he despised turning people or killing them. He didn't even like taking the life of an animal. Athena went out in search of a man that would take his place. Someone that she could count on. To do anything she asked him to with out a thought or regret. She found such a man coming out of a pub after a fight in the pub. She went up to him and seized him by his throat. She bit him and drank then she slit her wrist, and made him drink. Athena then asked him what his name was. He told her that his name was Ben. Athena said, well Ben tonight you have been reborn into darkness. So tonight you will be given a new name, from now on your name shall be Dimitrius. Come with me and I will get you some new clothes to wear. Then we will go out for a hunt and I will teach you all that I learned from my master Adrian. "Will I ever get to meet your master?" "No he is no longer a vampire. He is now just a warlock. He was turned back to the way he was before. When his maker was killed by demon hunters." Just as she said that Adrian and Dominique came flying by. The two black owls landed right in front of them. Then turned into Adrian and Dominique. Adrian looked at Athena then said, "I see that you have not changed at all, since we saw each other last. What ever happened to your old traveling companion Aineias and his bat?" "He had the demon hunters, kill him just like your precious Bernadette did." Adrian got very angry he flew over to her and grabbed her by the throat. Her feet were above the ground. He looked her in the eyes, and told her to never speak her name again ever! Then he dropped her on the ground, she came to her feet. She looked at him and said, "I see that you have not changed. You are just as you were; when you were one of us." Dominique told Dimitrius, not to look at her as his next victim. Spike was growling at him so he backed off. Athena told, Dominique that she would have been his first victim. Because he was turned that very night. And that was to be his first of many hunts. Dominique told, her to watch her step and her back. When she was around, because she was much stronger than she was. Adrian and Dominique flew off and went home for the rest of the night. Carrying Spike back with them. Armand and the others were also out for a nightly walk. Christine told them not to go down that path. Because she knew that there were two vampires on that path looking for prey. So the four of them took another path. Dimitrus spotted his very first victim. She was walking through the woods alone. She appeared to be lost. Dimitrus went to her and said, "I can help you find your way home." He looked her right in the eyes and then she closed hers. He bit her very softly, she fell into a deep sleep. When she came to he had her drink from his wrist. Athena was very pleased with his gift. She knew right there and then that she had picked the right man. To help her build her colony of vampires. Tomas said to Guinevere, "someone just got turned. We need to be on our toes so we can hopefully save the next one before it's to late." Guinevere told him, that they should bring Justin and Gabrielle with them the next time they go out at night. Christine said, "maybe we should bring the whole coven with us as well." Marcus, Nicole, Antonis and Dora were at the Blue Moon eating. While all of this was going on. Carol and Sara were waiting on the tables. In came Willa and Albert to have dinner and then go to a movie after words. Patricia, Victor, Charles and Kathrine were all ready at the movie theater watching the movie. Back at the caretakers house, Armand said; "we really will have to keep our eyes on those two." Tomas said, "your right about that; Adrian really trained her well." Just then Bernadette and Joesph showed themselves. Bernadette said, "Adrian was a very bad teacher. He did not teach me a damn thing at all about being a vampire! I had to learn all on my own," Guinevere said, "you only killed small animals. Then Willa put that frige in your room. Until you died and now you are a ghostly witch." Joesph said, "there's no reason to be stating the obvious." Christine said, "he is right we have a huge problem on our hands."

Dark Dynasty
Part 11

Athena & Dimitrus

They were right about Athena and Dimitrus. The two of them turned at least two victims. Each every night after Dimitrus became a vampire. And they killed almost the same amount as they turned. Christine and Guinevere called for a coven meeting. All of the witches in Carington Point were there. Even Bernadette's spirit was there. Victor and Patricia brought Justin and Gabrielle with them. Christine told them, that they needed all the help that they could find. Bernadette told them, that they would also need Adrian's; help to get rid of them both. Joesph said, "I hate myself for saying this but she is right. After all his is the one that made her, what she is a frickin bitch! So he should be the one that gets rid of her once and for all!" Bernadette's spirit left she went to get Adrian, Dominique and Spike. When she came back they all flew in together. Tomas said, "we will all stay here to night and go out in the morning to find their hiding place." Charles came in with Kathrine and said, "I hope that you have room for two more?" Armand said, "yes we do we really do need every one that wants to do their part to get rid of this bitch!" Marcus came in with Nicole and Carol. Even Antonis and Dora were there as well. Tomas said, "we all need to get some sleep. We will all go out in the morning, bright and early. And search for their den together as one big team." Just as they were getting ready to get some sleep for the night. There was a knock at the door, it was Willa and Albert. Tomas answered the door and let them in We were hoping that you might have room for at lest two more. We do come on in, we were all getting ready to get some sleep. Before we head out in the morning. Albert asked, "just what are they heading out to do in the morning?" Armand looked at Willa and said, "didn't you tell him just what we are here for?" No I wanted him, to hear it from Bernadette. Just what else it is we do with our powers besides casting spells. Bernadette looked at Albert and told him to sit down, before she told him why we were all there. He looked at her with the look of confusion and fear on his face. "We are here because we are going on a hunt for vampires. Which I myself once was, before I had Justin kill me. So that my spirit could be with Joseph's in the after life. Now I'm a ghostly witch. Adrian was also a vampire until we killed his maker. And now he is only an immortal warlock." Adrian said, "we are here to hunt down, and kill one of the vampires that I made; many years ago. She is far worse then I ever was." Armand looked right at his brother and said, "Adrian what about all of the victims, that you killed or turned. Before you were sent to hell. And that was before, you were returned; to the way you are now." There are also all of them that you turned even before that including Bernadette. And then there is the fact, that you also killed Joesph as well." Adrian looked at his brother and said, "I have changed for the better since I have returned to my former self. Brother dear and I can also thank Dominique for a lot of it as well. I am here to right a wrong not to be judged by you or anyone else. If you do not want or need my help then we will leave right now damn it!" Bernadette went over to Adrian and said, "we really need your help, you are the one that knows her best. You are the only one that would, know where she might be hiding at. So I am asking to please stay and help us get rid of her." "All right we will stay because you asked so nicely." Armand went over to him and said, "I'm sorry bro, but I thought that; Albert should know what he was getting himself into before he helps us." Adrian said, "your right he is new to all of this. He is also an officer of the law. So maybe he should not be here." Albert spoke up and said, "I'm not going anywhere as long as Willa is here. I know that she can take of herself because she is a witch. I am here to up hold the law and to make sure that no one gets hurt on my watch."

Tomas said, "then we all can agree, that we are all going out to get; rid of Athena, Dimitrus. And their clan of vampires once and for all. Before they can kill or turn anyone else."

Athena's Diary

I was Adrian's very first vampire bride. I was replaced by Bernadette and I hated them both because of it. I wanted to kill her but he would not let me. He sent me as far away as he possible could. I have waited for years to get my revenge, But when I finally found both of them. I found out that Adrian was no longer a vampire. And that he was now just a warlock. I also learned that Bernadette was now a ghostly witch. So I took my anger and revenge out on innocent people that I didn't even know.

Dark Dynasty
Part 12

The Finale

Early the next morning everyone in the caretakers house was armed. And as ready as they could be. For what possibly could be the biggest fight they ever had. Since the fight between the werewolves and the beasts. They were not sure who would die or who would come back alive. All they knew for sure, was that they had to rid their selves; of this evil bitch for ever. And everyone that she had turned. Especially Dimitrus because he is the next, one in line. To rule over the clan of vampires when Athena is dead. Guinevere said, "if we kill the two of them ,then the others may turn back; to the way they were before. Or they may stay as they are which is a vampire. Then we will have to kill them as well." Christine told, "them to stay together in two teams of 1o. Use only your thoughts to call upon each other for back up when you need to only." They went their separate ways. Albert made sure that he stayed close, to Willa because he felt safe; with her by his side. Bernadette and Joesph went with Willa and Albert. Adrian, Dominique and Spike went with Armand and Christine's group. Both groups ended up at the same place and at the same time. The sun had just started to come up, now was the perfect time to strike. They all went in together. The ones that knew just what to do opened all of the curtains to let in the sun light. Then they opened the coffins one by one, took their stakes; and placed them over their hearts. Took their hammers and hit the stakes as hard as they could. In tell they heard their last gasp of breath. Armand knew that there was, something very wrong with this whole thing. "We need to get out of here now! And burn this place to the ground! Guinevere knew he was right she said, "this is a trap and we all should get out of here right now! Adrian pick up Spike and lets all get the hell out of here!" They all got out safely then they burned the building to the ground. Adrian said, "I know where she is, she in the old castle just outside of town. Because she was the very first that I turned. She thought of me as the king of vampires. So she called herself my queenly wife." Armand said, "so ex king of the night, why didn't you live in a castle; like Count Dracula?" Adrian looked at his brother, and started to laugh then said; "dear brother this is not the time to be cracking jokes." They all headed toward the old castle where Athena and Dimitrus were. They had no idea what was in store for them when they got there. All they knew was that they had to kill both of them before the sun went down. Tomas said, "we have to hurry so that we can reach there before darkness falls." "Sara said, we will have to use our powers to get us there then."

So they all got into a big circle and began to chant. The next thing they knew they were right in front of the castle. Christine handed out cloaking capes for everyone even Albert and Spike. Then they all went in and split up into groups of ten again. Each group took a path, one path went east the other went wast. Guinevere's half found Dimitrus's part of the clan. She made it look like the sun was still up even though it was all most set. They opened his coffin and let the light hit right on him. His skin began to turn to ash. Tomas staked him before he could realize that the sun light was not real. And that the ashes were from a fireplace and that he was not turning to ash at all.

Christine's half found Athena's room. She did not want her group to go in with out her sister. She sent a message to Guinevere that they had found Athena. But that she did not think that they should go in with out her. Guinevere sent one back to her letting her know that Dimitus was dead. Told her to stay right where she was and that they would be there soon. When she got there they all went in together. Athena was waiting for them with what was left of her army of darkness. Athena was very angry she said, "I know why your here, and I know that over half; of my people are dead damn it! And that you killed Dimitrus! Why in the hell wont all of you show yourselves to me damn it! I want to see your faces when I kill all of you one at a time! The ones that I do not kill I will turn to renew my clan of the night." Bernadette told, everyone to keep their cloaking capes on know mater what happens. So they did just as she told them to do. Bernadette and Joesph were not wearing one because they are all ready dead. So they showed their selves to her. All of sudden the spirits of Darin and grandmother Guinevere showed up.

We are not going to let you harm, our family in any way; if we can help it you evil bitch! Along with the spirits of Keith and Rick in tow. Darin's spirit spoke, "I am here to keep you and your demon freaks from killing or turning my wife!" Athena Carol said, "you are out numbered you and your clan can not win this fight. Our combined powers will help us win and you know it."

"I will not give up with out a fight, even if we do lose. I will take as many, of you down with me as I can, So let the fight begin!" Fire balls were flying lightening was flashing and thunder was cracking! And bodies wore being tossed like rag dolls. Arrows were also flying through the air. With fire on the tip of the arrows. The vampires were screaming out in pain as they went up in flames and then vanished. All of them were dead but one Athena. She knew that all was lost so she vanished from the room. Adrian knew her well enough that he knew just where she would go to hide. He told Dominique that he was going to go after her alone. And that he cared for her to much to put her in harms way. He wanted her to take Spike home and that he would meet her there later. Dominique told him that she, was going to go with him and that was that. Armand told him that he would also go with him. Christine told, Armand she was not going to let him go with out her. Guinevere said to her sister, you are all the family I have left you are not going with out me! Bernadette told, Willa that they were all going to go after Athena. Willa I want you and Albert to go home now. Keep the capes to keep you both safe until the two of you get home. So the two of them left. The rest of them followed Adrian to the grave yard. To kill Athena before she turned anyone else. When they got there she had all ready turned a man and a woman. They knew that they could still take her life. Because the two of them were the only ones, that she had time to turn with out help. Adrian was still wearing the cape so it was very easy, to go up to her and stab her in the chest. The other two fell to the ground in pain. They asked to be killed, so Justin did as they asked him to. After everything was over they all went home. Knowing that everyone could sleep well at lest for now. They all held out hope, that their little town of Carington Point. Would be once again the quiet place that it once was.

Bernadette's Final Diary Entry

This is my last diary entry. I would like to tell you more about my life. As you all ready know I was named, after my mother's mum Bernadette. Her full name was Bernadette Demonte. I was never a mother, Joseph and I were robbed of that by Adrian. I still hate him for that. I am glad that Joseph and I are together again. I just wished that could have been in life, and not in the after life. Alisa and I lost our mother when she was hung for witch craft. Her name was Carlotta Demonte Stephanos. Our father moved us from Palermo Italy to Thebes Greece after our mother died. His name was Bernard Stephanos. I meant Joseph there we were married there. Our father died right after we were married. Joseph, Alisa and I moved to Carington Point in 1918. Shortly after we moved there Alisa married Joseph's first cousin and had Edward and 2 years later had Rachel.

Edward's Diary

I am Edward Cairnngton my sister Rachel and our children live in the the main house. On the Cairinngton estate in Cairnington Point. We run a textile plant, and a family run clothing store. My daughter Daniella can see and talk to spirits. And dabbles in witch craft, my daughter's mother aka ex wife. Married my sisters ex husband (or late husband). Or what ever in the hell you want to call him! My sister's son just got married. The poor sucker, I hope they will be happy and that it will last longer then mine did. I'm now living in the attic apartment. Where all of the spooks use to live. I can only hope that they are all gone. Because I moved up here to get some peace and quiet.

Linette and Angeline's Diary

We are the sisters, of Maiadis and Damius.. Like them we were born deformed beasts. Like Maladis (a k a Marcus) we were given a new lease on life. His friends transformed us into two beautiful young ladies. Which now shows to us that not all witches are evil. Unfortunately for our older brother, it's sadly to late to prove that to him. Because he was killed, to protect the innocent from his wrath.

Maladis a.k.a Marcus Carington

*I*should not be here, I have done nothing wrong. I only kill in self defense, I did not deserve to be entombed in a medial coffin ether. I was born this way, a gypsy witch put a curse on my mother; before I was born. My own father sold me to the gypsies. When I was old enough to work, they made me cleanup after them and their animals. I started to rebel and run away. So they would beat me and put me back in my cage, as a punishment. My bed was made out of dry leafs and an old blanket. And if I was thirsty they would give me a bowl of water to drink out of like a dog. The cage was placed where everyone could see me look at me point and laugh or scream and run away. One night I was sitting there hoping that someone would come by and let me out. When a young boy came by with the keys, in his hand and let me out. I thanked him and ran off as fast as I could. I tried not to be seen by anyone, while I was traveling from town to town. I only killed those that tried to kill me first. And that is why they entombed me. Because they thought that I was a threat to all mankind.

Thy Ignorance is a Crime

of Miss Fortunate Events

Extra Story
Thy Ignorance is a Crime
of Miss Fortunate Events

Detectives Meredith Simmons and Danek Mc Cole had just got back from Victoria B C. They were hoping to get some well deserved rest. When the phone rang it was their Captain Gillian Mc Moore. He was calling them into the office to talk, to them about a missing person. A man named Artemus Stratton, His wife Vera called. She told Arabella that he had been missing for 24 hrs. A woman named Shannon called and told her that she found a car on the road that looked like it had run out of gas. But the diver was not sitting in the car. And she did not see anyone, walking on the road into town to get gas. Caring a gas can in their hand. Arabella asked her if see saw a wallet or a jacket in the car? She said that there was no sign of life at all. What does the car look like? Danek asked Gillian. It's a chevy nova black four door. Danek, Meredith, and her dog went out and got into Danek's truck. They found the car just where the witness said it was. They decided to go into the woods to see if he might have gone the wrong way. When they got further into the woods they found him tied to a tree in nothing but his under clothes. He was unconscious and very cold to the touch. They took pictures of the crime scene. Danek untied him and put a blanket over him. Then put him in the truck. Then drove him to the hospital. Nurse Muron took him into an exam room. Dr. Mc Dempsey gave him a full exam. As Dr. Mc Dempsey was looking over Artemus he suddenly woke up and asked, "where in hell am I? And way am I here?" The doctor told him that he was at the hospital. The nurse came out of the room. And told Meredith and Danek that he was a wake. And that they could talk to him about what happened to him in the woods. They went in to ask him some questions about what happened to in the last 24 hrs. Artemus told them that all he could remember was that he ran out of gas just outside of town. And the last thing he could remember was falling asleep tied to the tree. He told them that until the dr. told him what his name was that he could not even remember it. He said. that the doc, told him that he was married and that her name is Vera. And that she is coming here to pick me up. "I'm still not sure if my name is Artemus Stratton or not, and that I'm really even married. Meredith asked him to close his eyes and try to go back in his mind. To see if he could recall anything at all about that night. He said, all he could recall was the smell of roses in the air. And a woman's voice telling him to fallow her into the woods. Danek said, "and so you did just what she asked you to do. She must have drugged you some how, and removed all of your clothing; except under clothes." Just as Danek said that in walked Vera. She was about to go in and yell at him. When Meredith pulled her aside. And told her, that he could not remember, anything at all not even her. Which means she must have drugged him. The doctor walked over and told Vera that Artemus would have to stay over night, so that they could take some tests. To find out just what kind of drugs she used on her husband. Dr. Mc Dempsey called the lab and asked Brian to come and pick up the lab work, and give it to Michaela. "Have her call me when she finds out what kind of drug or drugs this woman is using on her victims." Mean while Sorina was getting ready to go out in search of her next victim. As darkness fell she went out to find some one to toy with. She had decided to take the next one home with her. She came upon a man walking his dog. She did not drug this one as much as she did the first one. Because she wanted him to be able to walk. They got into her carriage and headed for her house. When they got there she took him to a room. And had him change into some bed clothes. Then drugged him and put him in a bed, tied him up and left him there. She took the dog with her watered and fed it. Back at the hospital Danek asked Dr. Mc Dempsey if he thought, that the woman; might of used a hypnotic drug of some kind. Dr. Mc Dempsey told him, that it might very well be the case. But if it is we still do not know which one she may have used. As they were talking. The phone at the desk ring, the nurse answered it. "It's for you Dr. it is Michaela from the lab." She handed him the phone, Michaela told him, "that she found out that one of the drugs she used was chloroform. I still do not know, what the other one is that she used is yet." But that she would let him know, as soon as she found out what it was." He thanked her then hung up. Danek asked him what she had told him. The Doctor told them that, one of the drugs she used on him; was chloroform to put him to sleep. But she does not know what the other one is yet. Meredith came over and said, "I know what the other drug is. I just got off the phone with coroner Dr Beterson. He told me that it sounds like she may have used belladonna on him. Danek asked, her as they were leaving, "how does she give them the drugs?" Meredith told him, that she uses poison rings. "She blows the belladonna in their face. The ring with the chloroform in it she places under their nose." They went back to the office to tell their captain. What they found out about the suspect. He told them to go home and get some sleep. While they were on their way home. Sorina was making the young mans life a living nightmare. She made him think that there was someone in the room with him. When he was all a lone in the room. She had not given him anything to eat or drink in 12 hrs. She was taking every good care of the dog how ever. That night she went out again, and this time they will find the young man dead. She found Rico Maritnez walking into town. To get water for his radiator. Sorina lured him into the woods. And she did the same thing to him that she did to the first man. Only she killed this one by giving him a deadly dose of belladonna. After she left him she went home and let the other man and his dog go. To wonder around the woods dazed until someone finds him. Or until he some how finds his way, out of the woods and; to the road leading to town. That night a couple was walking through the woods with their dog. They suddenly came upon the body tied to the tree. They ran out of there as fast as they could. When they came out they stopped to catch their breath. As they were standing there a cop car came by. They pulled over and asked them what was wrong. They told them that there was a body back in the woods. One officer stayed with the young lady. The other one went with the young man back into the woods. Where he showed him where the body was. They went back to the car, where the officer called the coroner; and told them to come and pick up the body. They stayed there until the coroners van came. To pick up the body and take pictures of the crime scene. The officers drove the couple home. They got a call while heading back to the station. That a witness saw a man in bed clothes walking his dog in the woods. The man looked dazed and scared, she said I tried to talk to him; but he ran away from me. So I had my husband go after him he got him to stop running. He brought him to the hospital. Meredith and Danek were called by Dr, Mc Dempsey. To come and talk to the man in one the hospital rooms. So they came to talk to him as the doctor ask them to. He told them the same thing that Artemus told them. Danek asked him, if she had an accent? He said that she had a french one. Meredith asked him, if he could remember where her house was? He said no I can't, "all I know is that I was there for 24 hrs. And that she did not give me anything to eat or drink. She didn't even let me got to the bathroom. She took better care of my dog then she did me. The bitch tried to make me go mad. By making think that I was seeing and hearing things that were not even there." "So you can't tell use what she looks like at all,?" Danek asked. No I can't I was drugged the whole time I was there. Meredith asked, "how did you escape then?" "She let me leave I guess she got tired of toying with my head." After they left the hospital, they headed to the coroners office. To talk to Doc. Beterson about Rico Martitanz and how he died. When they got there he told them that he was given an over dose of belladonna. They were also told that he had two more bodies. That came in and that they had died the same way that Rico did. Danek asked him, if he knew what their names were? William told them that the killer, or some one mailed their wallets to his office. There was no return address on the box that they came in. Meredith asked him if she could see their drivers licenses. The names on them were, Radley Mason and Damion Grossfield. Danek asked William, "if either one of them were married?" He told them that nether one were married. They thanked him for his time and left. They drove around the woods trying to find Sorina they finally came to a house that they thought mite be hers. So they got out of the truck and looked around the grounds. Then they decided to go in side. When they got there they looked around. They went from room to room. They came to the room where the young man was kept. Kallie found his clothes and his shoes. She also found his wallet. The name on the drivers license, is Stan Rolland. The only thing they did not find was Sorina. There wasn't even any sign of her carriage. Or the horses that she used to pull the carriage. It was almost like she had vanished into thin air. As they were getting ready to leave. Meredith asked Danek, "what about the driver of the carriage?" Danek said, you want to know where he is; if he is still here or if he left with her. All of a sudden they heard Kallie, barking at a door in the carriage house. So they went and pride the door open with a crowbar. And there they found the carriage driver all tied up and gagged. They took him out of the room. Then they put him in the truck. And headed for the hospital, to drop him off and give Stan his things. After they checked him in at the desk. They went to Stan's room where they had Kallie. Take the bag with Stan's belongings to him. Then they went back to the station to tell Gillian everything that they knew about the case of The Phantom Poison Killer (a k a Sorina). The three of them went home hoping to finally get that rest that they really needed. When they got home their cat Ember was waiting for them on the sofa. As for Sorina she must have grown tired of their little town. She decided to move on to another one. And a new carriage driver, which also means more victims. For the next towns police officers to deal with. That means for Meredith and Danek more new crimes and new suspects. They are hoping for a little down time.

Sorina

I toy with my victims
It's all a game to me
Then when I grow
weary of them and
The thrill is gone
I either set them free
dazed and confused
Or I end their suffering
alive or dead it doesn't
matter to me I will
move on like a
Phantom in the night

Sorina's Diary

My name is Sorina, I am the infamous Phantom poison killer. I choose my victims selectively. I toy with non violent ignorant ones, to me it is a game. As for the ones I feel are not worthy and have committed crimes. They unfortunately meet their demise to me I consider it justice. The reason I am called the Phantom poison killer is they can not catch me. And the method I use a poison ring less violent and no blood. So in a way I am like a phantom I move on undetected and unnoticed.

Ignorance is Not Bliss

The air was clean and now
it is brown we could plant
our food in the ground and
now we have to plant it in
a green house we use to use
natural ways to heat our
homes and now use man
made heat the water was
blue and clear and now
it is black the sea was
once beautiful and now
murky the sea life is dying
and no body cares they
would rather kill each othre
and our once upon a
time beautiful home
rather than try to save
it because all the think
about is greed and fame
What a shame!

The Ponderance of Life

To or not to? That is the question
To ponder life away and do nothing
Or to go forward and live your dreams
Or let them go by with out even trying
To give up with out a fight or to try
With all your might To love or to hate
To live with or with out a mate what
a lot to contemplate when your born
everything is done for you and then
you grow up and do everything for
yourself no one can help you but you so
Go for what you want and do your
best and if you fall get up and try again
And never ask yourself the question to do
or not to do? Because the answer is if
at first you don't succeed try, try again

Ariana C. Dolan

Save Our Mother

Mother earth is screaming and no one
Is listening to her she is dying before
She is completely gone for good please
Help her stay with us before it's to late
Mans greed is killing her and all that
She as made we are not the only ones
Suffering her animals are dieing too
Father sky is crying fire water tears
We must stop all of this madness
And all of killing before it is to late
We must clean up our home before
it dies So please save our home
before it is to late divided we will
falter together we will make a
Deference so please help our mother
before it is to late Mother earth is
Screaming!!

A BOOK OF THREE TALES

Muron Foley